VIRAGO
MODERN CLASSICS

A Far Cry from Kensington

When Mrs Hawkins tells Hector Bartlett he is a *'pisseur de copie'*, that he 'urinates frightful prose', little does she realise the repercussions. Holding that 'no life can be carried on satisfactorily unless people are honest' she refuses to retract her judgement, and loses not one, but two much-sought-after jobs in publishing.

Now, years older, successful, and happily a far cry from Kensington, Mrs Hawkins looks back over the dark days that followed, in which she was embroiled in a mystery involving anonymous letters, quack remedies, blackmail and suicide.

'My admiration for Spark's contribution to world literature knows no bounds. She was peerless, sparkling, inventive and intelligent – the crème de la crème'
Ian Rankin

D1497678

THE WRITER

Muriel Spark (1918–2006) was born in Edinburgh. She wrote many successful novels, including *The Prime of Miss Jean Brodie, Memento Mori, Loitering with Intent, A Far Cry from Kensington* and *Symposium*, as well as poems, short stories, plays, biographies and children's books. For her long career of literary achievement Muriel Spark won international praise and many awards. She was given an honorary doctorate of Letters from a number of universities, London, Edinburgh and Oxford among these, and was made a Dame of the British Empire in 1993.

THE DESIGNER

Lucienne Day graduated from the Royal College of Art in 1940. Her career in design spans over sixty years. With her husband Robin Day she pioneered the post-war revival of design and manufacture, and extended the boundaries of modern design, enjoying international recognition. Her best-known textile design 'Calyx' is used on the cover of this book. It was designed for Heal's and launched at the Festival of Britain in 1951. It was hailed for capturing the spirit of the age and subsequently received the coveted International Design Award of the American Institute of Decorators.

ALSO BY MURIEL SPARK

A FAR CRY FROM
KENSINGTON

MURIEL SPARK

INTRODUCED BY ALI SMITH

VIRAGO

This hardback edition published in 2008 by Virago Press

7 9 10 8 6

First published in Great Britain in 1988 by Constable and Company

A CIP catalogue record for this book
is available from the British Library.

ISBN 978-1-84408-527-9

Typeset in Goudy by M Rules
Printed and bound in Great Britain by
Clays Ltd, Elcograf S.p.A.

Papers used by Virago are from well-managed forests
and other responsible sources.

MIX
Paper from
responsible sources
FSC® C104740

Virago Press
An imprint of
Little, Brown Book Group
Carmelite House
50 Victoria Embankment
London EC4Y 0DZ

An Hachette UK Company
www.hachette.co.uk

www.virago.co.uk

INTRODUCTION

Can you decide to think? – Yes, you can. You can put your mind to anything most of the time. You can sit peacefully in front of a blank television set, just watching nothing; and sooner or later you can make your own programme much better than the mass product. It's fun, you should try it. You can put anyone you like on the screen, alone or in company, saying and doing what you want them to do, with yourself in the middle if you prefer it that way.

What do we do with our lives? How do we employ ourselves? How do we view our pasts, and more, how do we survive them to inhabit our futures? And what do we do if those pasts keep us awake at night? *A Far Cry from Kensington* is one of Muriel Spark's most liberating, liberated and meditative novels. Spark is a writer who can take the meditative and make it mercurially funny, playful and mischievous; alongside the grim 'cry' at the core of this novel there's a force of fun, and a force of calm light-heartedness in its analysis of the creative process in the light of free will, imagination, truth and history.

First published in 1988, *A Far Cry from Kensington* is a conscious exercise in looking back – it is a novel that announces its own preoccupied insomnia. But its insomnia is unexpectedly pleasant, a beloved wakefulness in the 'sweet waking hours of the night' – as if the usual dark night of the soul has been replaced by something much, much lighter. We begin in the present, or what we might call the future, intimate with its narrator Mrs Hawkins, who is awake in her bed, listening, in the silence, to the noise of the mid-1950s, thirty years ago. In her reverie she is a publishing assistant living in a shabby, decent rooming-house in down-at-heel Kensington (how things change over time!), run by Milly, an Irish landlady of great kindness and frankness. And she is literally larger than life, large enough in a post-war time of rationing and utilitarian discomfort to suggest a comforting abundance to everyone who simply looks at her.

Mrs Hawkins has a lot on her plate, as it were, which is something she learns practically and literally to deal with in the course of the novel. She has simply spoken the truth, out loud; she has told a rather bad writer called Hector Bartlett, to his face, exactly what she thinks – that he's a bad writer, a '*pisseur de copie*'. 'It means that he pisses hack journalism, it means that he urinates frightful prose.' Bartlett happens to be having an affair with a famous novelist, Emma Loy (whose character is a shining piece of sardonic creation by Spark). Emma Loy has a lot of sway in the book world – and this particular London is full of people surreally chasing jobs in the publishing industry; part of the novel's high entertainment is its satire of the book business, as if a job in publishing is like a golden ticket for entry to life itself. 'Jobs in publishing, Mrs Hawkins, are very hard to come by. You might bear that in mind. I could put in a word for you in many quarters. Only you must, simply must, retract.' The power struggle is swift. Pretty soon Mrs Hawkins is out of a job.

Over at the rooming-house, 'from Wanda's room came a long, loud, high-pitched cry which diminished into a sustained, distant and still audible ululation.' Wanda, the Polish dress-maker, has started receiving anonymous threats. 'We, the Organisers, have our eyes on you.' Everyone at the rooming-house suspects everyone else; everything polarises down to the single question – are you a friend or an enemy? But Mrs Hawkins, eyes like the hawk in her name, notices how cheap the threatening letters look, how fake, like a deliberate literary performance of poor quality; an attempt at parody, if a lame one. Is Wanda guilty? Of what? Why has she, like many others in this slim, far-reaching novel, fallen so completely for the hype about a mesmerising, modern yet medieval-sounding contraption called the Box, which, its proponents claim, has the power to cure all ills? And what exactly is the Box, with its 'radionic' power in the new radioactive age, its special resonance for the radio and TV generations reading this book in the 1980s?

When these three different farcical stories come together, Mrs Hawkins finds herself at the centre of a cheap detective mystery, on the one hand, and on the other a set of metaphysical tests concerning power and truth: 'No life can be carried on satisfactorily unless people are honest.' Meanwhile, post-war London comes back to life, 'strange grasses and wild herbs had sprung up where the war-demolished houses had been', because in many ways this is a novel distinctly about revival, particularly about the aftermath of the war, how such trauma can be healed by its walking wounded. *A Far Cry from Kensington* is, in the end, a beautiful – and still suitably utilitarianly 'sober' – celebration of a whole new blossoming. This wonderful blossoming is the real mystery, in a novel which doesn't just sort the frauds from the true, but also the good frauds from the bad frauds, and which becomes a conscious act of revitalisation, not just of a city, but of its people and also their potential literature.

A Far Cry from Kensington was Spark's eighteenth novel and, incidentally, takes place around the time when, in her own life, she was living in London and first writing her own fiction; her first novel, *The Comforters*, was completed in the mid-fifties and published in 1957. This particular time in her life is very entertainingly dealt with in her only volume of autobiography, *Curriculum Vitae* (1992), a book she published four years after this novel and whose voice, wry and calm, witty and sharp, is very close to the voice of *A Far Cry's* narrator.

Spark had spent the latter war years working in intelligence for the Foreign Office. When the war ended she made a career move that must have seemed very farcical indeed after such work; she took a post at the Poetry Society, editing its periodical, *Poetry Review*, and by all accounts enduring a series of mini wars, battling with every mad faction imaginable in the London literary world. After this she took a position three days a week with Peter Owen, whom she writes of in

Curriculum Vitae as, 'a young publisher who was interested in books by Cocteau, Hermann Hesse, Cesare Pavese. It was a joy to proof-read the translations of such writers. I was secretary, proof-reader, editor, publicity girl . . . in the office at 50 Old Brompton Road, with one light bulb, bare boards on the floor, a long table which was the packing department.' Much of her Poetry Society experience slipped in to *Loitering with Intent*, her marvellous novel written seven years before *A Far Cry from Kensington*, which dealt with the years just prior to those depicted here. With its lambasting of literary vicious circles and all their bombast and fakery, and by dint of its sheer post-war joyousness, *Loitering with Intent* can be seen as a sister volume, the bright noon to this 'wide-eyed midnight' of a novel.

But in Spark's work the lightness of things is always a serious business, and a literary vicious circle is likely to be one of the worst forms of viciousness, since she is an artist profoundly drawn to a morality in the art process, and especially to the function of fiction in the real world. For Spark, who converted to Roman Catholicism at about the same time as she wrote her first fiction (and consequently at about the same time as *A Far Cry* is set), the religious process, the writing process, the process of simply living and the processes of art are inextricably intertwined. Her belief system gifted her a 'balanced regard for matter and spirit',[1] as she called it, and a vision of all our realities, all our 'real' histories, as a kind of parallel fictional work; and this gives the recurring notions in her work of the relationships between fiction, truth and lies, between real and fake, between author, authority and free will, a particular slant.

Here the trivial, intimate history of the novel apes the reality whose setting it is, in a plot that resembles a mini Cold War, a mini descent into 1950s post-war paranoia. Where the novel's surface is scattered with authentic references that make obvious links between fiction and real time ('Billy Graham; Senator McCarthy; Colonel Nasser; . . . *Lucky Jim*'), where its general theme might be said to be a people getting back into shape in the post-war years, its subtext is Spark's endless preoccupation: the 'supernatural process going on under the surface and within the substance of all things'.[2] The novel's own preoccupation is moral – the makings of good and bad – in this case, what makes a good or a bad writer, in a novel where gratuitous viciousness and powermongering, and 'bad' and 'untrue' writing, come together as the same thing. This is a book that knows itself to be a book – and is always announcing its status to its reader. 'I offer this advice', our narrator says, 'without fee; it is included in the price of the book,' a book very much about the act of narrative skill, about the uses of foreground, background, foresight, hindsight, or the basics of narrative structure. Mrs Hawkins, our 'scrupulous' proof-reader and editor, almost suggests this novel is a case-book for those who would wish to write well.

The book's subject is the thoughtful self, the self making sense, from an objective distance, of the meanings of both silence and voice. Its first refrain is the pained cry of the lost, wounded woman at the centre of its plot, and to some extent also Mrs Hawkins's own silent cry, which readers learn of when they come upon the story of her war-marriage. Its other, more pervasive, refrain is much sweeter, and arises from emotional distance, from the meditative future itself which will, it is promised, simply put the past into its proper context: 'I came to realise the answer later,' as Mrs Hawkins repeatedly says. 'I'm a great believer in providence,' Spark herself wrote. 'It's not quite fatalism, but watching until you see the whole picture emerge.'[3]

Above all, this is a fiction about what happens when you speak the plain truth out loud, how to survive the consequence, and the damage that happens to those taken in by, convinced by, the opposite of truth. It asks us not just to sense that we're being watched (in both the cheap 1950s paranoia plot as well as in a much larger metaphysical context), but more, to watch ourselves and, like Mrs Hawkins, to be ready to change, to change our own bad habits, to put ourselves blithely to rights. This blitheness is the key to survival in a novel in which the bruised, haunting dark of the past is ever present, but dealt with, as it were, with a combination of unsentimental affection and satisfying, score-settling wit – a perfect model of what critic Ruth Whittaker calls Spark's 'aesthetic of detachment' and, in the form of this novel, a prelude to every kind of revitalisation.

Spark often takes South London – and not the north of the city, which is the usual literary stamping-ground of novelists – as her subject in her books about the city. She likes to reveal alternatives. She comes, after all, to this most English of narratives, shot through with its references to the Brontës, Dickens and Forster, from a quite alternative position, for this most European of English novelists is a Scottish novelist, gifted in a particular otherness of authority, brought up between the wars in Edinburgh, where she 'imbibed, through no particular mentor, but just by breathing the informed air of the place, its haughty and remote anarchism. I can never now suffer from a shattered faith in politics and politicians, because I never had any.'[4]

This novel is about other faiths entirely. 'Can you decide to think?' This permissive education in the art of thinking, this laughing history of post-war literary London, this pensive and merry laying of old ghosts, is a book that knows its mere place as a book, and argues back about the importance of truth and art, and truth in art, with every fictive bone in its body. Masquerading as a chatty, realist piece of fiction, it is another revelation, as each of her novels is, of the far-reaching after effects of language well-used. 'That cry, that cry,' the far cry at its core is both idiomatic and actual, painful then distanced, examined and understood, by means of the Sparkian balance of artifice and truth. It all adds up to something huge – a sprightly philosophical rejection of twentieth-century angst, with all the carefree carefulness, all the far-reaching economy, all the merciless, sharp mercy, that characterise the art of Spark.

Ali Smith, 2008

Notes

1 Muriel Spark, from her article on Proust, 'The Religion of an Agnostic', quoted in *Muriel Spark* by Peter Kemp (London: Elek, 1974).

2 Muriel Spark, *The Mandelbaum Gate* (London: Harmondsworth, Penguin Books, 1967), p.199.

3 Muriel Spark, 'My Conversion', *Twentieth Century*, Autumn 1961, pp.58–63, p.63.

4 Muriel Spark, 'What Images Return', from *Memoirs of a Modern Scotland*, ed. Karl Miller (London: Faber, 1970), pp.151–53, p.153.

1

So great was the noise during the day that I used to lie awake at night listening to the silence. Eventually, I fell asleep contented, filled with soundlessness, but while I was awake I enjoyed the experience of darkness, thought, memory, sweet anticipations. I heard the silence. It was in those days of the early 'fifties of this century that I formed the habit of insomnia. Insomnia is not bad in itself. You can lie awake at night and think; the quality of insomnia depends entirely on what you decide to think of. Can you decide to think? – Yes, you can. You can put your mind to anything most of the time. You can sit peacefully in front of a blank television set, just watching nothing; and sooner or later you can make your own programme much better than the mass product. It's fun, you should try it. You can put anyone you like on the screen, alone or in company, saying and doing what you want them to do, with yourself in the middle if you prefer it that way.

At night I lay awake looking at the darkness, listening to the silence, prefiguring the future, picking out of the past the scraps I had overlooked, those rejected events which now came to the foreground, large and important, so that the weight of destiny no longer bore on the current problems of my life, whatever they were at the time (for who lives without problems every day? Why waste the nights on them?).

Often, it is a far cry from Kensington and the early 1950s, this scene of my night-watch. But even now when I return to London, to Kensington, and have paid the taxi and been greeted by the people waiting there, and have telephoned the friends and opened the mail, that night I find again my hours of sweet insomnia and know that it is a far cry from that Kensington of the past, that Old Brompton Road, that Brompton Road, that Brompton Oratory, a far cry. My thoughts of the night dwell often on those past thoughts of the night in the same way that my daily life at the time has a certain bearing on what I do now.

It was 1954. I was living in furnished rooms in a tall house in South Kensington. I was startled, some years ago, by a friend's referring to 'that rooming-house near South Kensington Underground you used to stay in'. Milly, the owner, would have denied indignantly that it was a rooming-house, but I suppose that is what it was.

Milly was sixty years of age, a widow. She is now well over ninety, and still very much Milly.

The house was semi-detached, and on the detached side was separated from its neighbour by no more than three feet. There were eighteen houses on each side of the street, of identical pattern. The wrought-iron front gates led up a short path, with a patch of gravel and flower-beds on either side and lined with speckled laurel bushes, to a front door which bore two panes of patterned glass. All Milly Sanders' tenants had a key to the front door which led into a small entrance hall. Milly herself occupied the ground floor. On the right, as you came in, was a hall-stand with a mirror, some coat-pegs, and a place for umbrellas; on one of its flat surfaces stood the telephone. On the left was Milly's best room, with a bow window, used only for visitors. Ahead was the staircase leading to the tenants' landings, and, to the left of the staircase, a short passage leading to Milly's sitting-room, kitchen, bedroom and its adjoining conservatory and her back garden which was good and sizeable for a London house. These streets had been built for merchant families of the past century.

Upstairs on the first floor was a bathroom and furnished rooms let to two single tenants and a couple. In the front bed-sitting-room, which also had a bow window and a small kitchen adjacent, lived the couple, Basil Carlin and his wife, Eva, both approaching forty and without children. Eva was a part-time infant-school teacher. Basil, by his own definition, was an engineering accountant. The Carlins were unusually quiet. Once they were locked in their room no sound ever issued, even after midnight when the natural noises of the house had ended for the day.

Next door to the Carlins was a large bedroom looking out into the garden. It had a wash-basin and a gas-ring with the usual dark steel box beside it with slots for pennies and for shillings. Here lived and worked Wanda, the Polish dress-maker whose capacity for suffering verged on rapacity. But Wanda Podolak was generous of heart even though she could never admit to an instant of happiness. She had many visitors, some clients – her ladies, she called them – volubly having their dresses fitted, some compatriot friends, some of whom she described as enemies. Most of her visitors came from six o'clock in the evening onwards, after their hours of work the clients being given preference over the friends and enemies, who had to wait on the landing till the fittings should be over. When Wanda entertained she didn't put away her work; the buzz of her sewing-machine went on intermittently together with the sonorous Polish voices of the men, the clamour of the women and the clatter of cups and saucers as tea was prepared. The Polish conversations seemed all the louder for being unintelligible, to anyone passing Wanda's door.

At the far end of the first landing was a smaller room occupied by Kate Parker, a twenty-five-year-old district nurse, small, dark, plump, with round black bird-like eyes and white gleaming teeth. She was a cockney. She seemed to give off vibrations of vigour and certainly she had great courage. Kate was frequently out for the evening or away on a job, but on the few nights she was at home she cleaned her room. She was very thorough and eager about her cleaning, indeed about everybody's house-cleaning; when she entered anyone else's room, for a cup of tea or to take their temperature, she would often say, politely, 'Your room's nice and clean.' If she failed to say this, it meant that your room wasn't clean. Kate detested germs, the work of the Devil. So on the evenings when she was at home she would haul her furniture out on the landing and scrub her linoleum with Dettol. The furniture, too, would have been scrubbed with disinfectant had it not been the landlady's property. Milly, long-suffering though she was, had objected to her table, chairs and bed being so much as wiped with a cloth impregnated with the stuff; it was enough, she said, that the house smelt of hospital after Kate's energetic cleaning. She gave Kate some lavender wax to clean her furniture with. It was impossible not to know that Kate was at home for the evening by the bumping and dragging of the furniture on to the landing, and the mixed reek of lavender and disinfectant. Kate vowed that when she had the money saved up, and a place of her own, it would be furnished with white-painted washable wood. Kate was strict and proud about her savings; they went into the Post Office. She kept in a cupboard in her room a series of little boxes with ready money in them. They were respectively marked 'electricity', 'gas', 'bus-fares', 'lunches', 'phone' and 'sundries'. Kate manicured her nails very carefully before going to bed, after the cleaning and hauling was over. She laid out her clothes for the morning with extra neatness. She would sometimes accept a drink, a sherry or a whisky, before going to bed, but always with a solemn sigh, as if to convey that she shouldn't really be taking the stuff, it might lead to ruin.

The floor above was where I lived in an attic room with a slanting ceiling. A stove and sink were installed; there was a built-in shower in the corner and under the slanting roof a deep, low cupboard.

On this floor was a communal lavatory and two other rooms, one occupied by young Isobel, who had a telephone of her own in her room so that she could ring her Daddy in Sussex every evening; it was only on this condition that Isobel had been allowed to come to London to work as a secretary. Sometimes Isobel would spend an entire evening on the telephone, not only to her Daddy but to her large acquaintance, and her voice trilled and sang through the thin walls with the cadences and saga of her daily doings.

The other room on the attic floor, smaller still, looked out on the garden. It was occupied by a medical student, William Todd, whose auditory effects were achieved by his wireless, frequently switched on to the classical music of the Third Programme. He studied better that way, he claimed.

Sometimes I had a party, and I suppose that gave evidence of my tenancy. Apart from that I was fairly quiet when I wasn't out for the evening. But generally when I was at home I would go downstairs and talk to Milly. Even down there in Milly's ground-floor rooms, there was frequently a din, for repairs and odd jobs to the house had to be done in the evening by a Mr Twinny who lived a few doors away. The reason Mr Twinny came to hammer and scrape after his own day's work was done was that Milly's economy didn't run to contractors or daytime workmen. Mr Twinny papered walls, with the paper laid out on a trestle work-table while Milly prepared the flour-and-water paste and brought to Mr Twinny the gelatinous size that he plastered over the paper. Or he would be unchoking a drain, with a clatter of tools, while Milly's television resounded, and I sat watching, drinking tea.

Milly, like everyone else in the house or in my office, never used my first name. Although I was a young woman of twenty-eight I was generally known as Mrs Hawkins. This seemed so natural to me and was obviously so natural to those around me that I never, at the time, thought of insisting otherwise. I was a war-widow, Mrs Hawkins. There was something about me, Mrs Hawkins, that invited confidences. I was abundantly aware of it, and indeed abundance was the impression I gave.

I was massive in size, strong-muscled, huge-bosomed, with wide hips, hefty long legs, a bulging belly and fat backside; I carried an ample weight with my five-foot-six of height, and was healthy with it. It was, of course, partly this physical factor that disposed people to confide in me. I looked comfortable. Photographs of the time show me with a moon-face, two ample chins and sleepy eyes. These are black-and-white photos. Taken in colour they would have shown my Rubens quality of flesh, eyes, skin. And I was Mrs Hawkins. It was not till later, when I decided to be thin, that right away I noticed that people didn't confide their thoughts to me so much, neither men nor women. As an aside, I can tell you that if there's nothing wrong with you except fat it is easy to get thin. You eat and drink the same as always, only half. If you are handed a plate of food, leave half; if you have to help yourself, take half. After a while, if you are a perfectionist, you can consume half of that again. On the question of will-power, if that is a factor, you should think of will-power as something that never exists in the present tense, only in the future and the past. At one moment you have decided to do or refrain from an action and the next moment you have already done or refrained; it is the only way to deal with will-power. (Only under sub-human stress does willpower live in time present but that is a different discourse.) I offer this advice without fee; it is included in the price of this book.

However all that may be, in the year 1954 I was comfortable in my fatness, known as a 'wonderful woman' although I had never done anything wonderful at all. I was admired for my largeness and that all-motherly look. A young woman who I imagine was older than myself once got up in a bus to offer

7

me a seat. I declined. She insisted. I realized she thought I was pregnant and accepted graciously. I enjoyed universal affection. I was Mrs Hawkins.

Between eleven o'clock and midnight the house gradually fell hushed and finally mute. On a few occasions the people in the house next door, a young Cypriot who described his occupation as vendor, and his English wife and sister-in-law, would decide to go out into their garden to have a row, or, as they called it when apologizing next day, a bit of an argument. These were all-night occasions, but they were rare. Generally by midnight the last lavatory chain would be pulled – 'That's Basil,' said Milly – and the house slept.

I lay in bed absorbing the stillness. The silence was actual, it was beautiful to my ears, all the more that in my inward ear I heard again the past day's sounds. Now that they were mute, I could put their sense together. And so, one of the night-thoughts out of many that I recall now, began with my waking to actually enjoy and almost hear that silence with which I have begun my story. My job was the noisiest I have ever known and in due time I will describe it. I say now that the silence that I woke to recalled to my mind another silence of my childhood while visiting relatives in Africa: I had been taken by car from Bulawayo to the Victoria Falls. Nature was still in the heat of the day. At a certain point, nearing the luxuriant forest of the Zambesi river, a deeper silence fell that made me realize that the previous silence had been illusory.

*

Milly had met her husband, John Sanders, in her native Cork early in the twentieth century when he was a soldier garrisoned there. Milly's mother was a widow who kept a corner shop of general goods, with two marble-topped tables at which ginger-pop and lemonade were served. John Sanders, a young sergeant, came frequently to buy his cigarettes and to chat. One day he asked Milly to a dance. Milly, behind the counter, looked at her mother, who nodded. The nod meant 'Yes, you can go,' as Milly explained to me.

Milly's narrative skill was considerable. Once, I told her so; she looked at me in such bewilderment, such doubt whether I was serious or in some way suggesting the stories were not true, that I never again complimented her on her style. I just listened, and noted how she brought a scene to life by a chance descriptive detail in the right place and by that graphic and right placing of words which most of the Irish excel at. She had no Irish blarney, she never exaggerated. I could listen to Milly for hours.

When I first knew her she was a very pretty woman of sixty, with thick shining silver hair and fine features. I think she had probably been a beauty, but she was embarrassed by any compliments about her looks.

Her bedroom was unheated and so she liked to undress and prepare for bed before the fire in her sitting-room, a partitioned part of the kitchen; but to do this she always turned off the television; she wouldn't for the world undress in front of an actor in a play, an announcer, or one of the ministers of religion who uttered his few comfortable words at the end of the day.

Nor would Milly be seen walking with a man. She would

certainly stop in the street to speak to a neighbouring male and would accompany a man she knew from the front door to his car, waving him good-bye. But she wouldn't walk down the street or cross the road with him. She had been widowed ten years. She followed some rule of her early days, I imagined.

Once in the course of conversation I became aware that Milly, who had borne three children, was under the fixed impression that you could not conceive a child unless you had experienced an orgasm – she called it 'that feeling'. I didn't argue. I didn't even draw any conclusion about Milly's marital life, and on the question whether she thought, reversely, that an orgasm inevitably produced a child, I kept my peace.

My office was in a converted Queen Anne house, now pulled down to make way for a sheer squared-off piece of real-estate off St James's Street. It was the Ullswater and York Press, known generally as the Ullswater Press, one of those small publishing houses which had barely survived the austerities of war-time, such as the rationing of paper supplies, the shortage of English printers, the lack of transport to carry the books from printers abroad; it had only kept going because the public was avid for books, especially the serious kind of books that the Ullswater Press provided. Then, as now, all jobs in publishing were greatly sought after, and, perhaps consequently, poorly paid. It was here, on the first floor, where the big general office was situated, that all the noise of the day went on. This room, which I imagine must have once been two interleading drawing-rooms, accommodated an editorial department at one end and a general sorting, post and packing section at the other. In between were three desks and a row of cabinets where the typing and filing went on; the two girls employed in these activities were sometimes joined by Cathy, the book-keeper, who would bring her bundles of bills from the accountant's room upstairs when he wanted to be alone or to receive a visitor in private.

In these months, the last of the firm of Ullswater and York before it failed, the accountant often wanted his privacy. When he sent Cathy down to us we speculated among ourselves who the visitor might be. Somebody ominous. Cathy, who had been in the firm far longer than any of us, wouldn't say. 'Is it the bailiffs at last, Cathy?' No answer. She was aged somewhere between fifty and seventy, with a puckered, reddish face, a balding head perhaps due to frequent dyeing, and spectacles with the thickest lenses I have ever seen, before or since. Cathy would bend her head with its few strands of hair, reddish and grey at the roots, black at the tips, over her bills, muttering to herself until we brought her a cup of tea with a biscuit in the saucer, whereupon she would look up with a smile of gratitude far more than was called for. Cathy's voice when she spoke above the existing din was a crackle of broken English. She had been in a German concentration camp in the 'thirties, and had got away.

The name of the firm, Ullswater and York, had no geographical connotation. There was a Mr Ullswater and a Mr York, partners. Two other directors and shareholders had joined the firm. Mr Ullswater, by far the elder of the partners, had now almost retired. He spent his days in the country, turning up once a month for a directors' meeting. He wore a bowler hat and a tweed suit, in winter a grey coat. He would arrive in a taxi, tall, white-haired, large-faced and amiable, climbing the stairs with a leisurely air. But he always left in a hurry, marching off as quickly as possible round the corner to his club. Martin York was a round-faced, square-cut man of about forty.

I never got my last week's wages. They owe me seven pounds, 1954 valuation. The noise in our general office might well have been due to an unconscious desire on our part to keep the devils away, after the practice of primitive tribes. The devils were to come in the end and Martin York was to go to prison for multiple forgeries and other types of fraud, but we employees, although we knew that the firm was rocky, did not as yet foresee quite so drastic a near future. We thought merely that we would soon have to find another job. In the meantime we got on with the jobs we had.

The shorthand-typist was called Ivy, a tall girl fresh from the secretarial college. Mary, the filing clerk, was a sixteen-year-old who had come straight from school. The packer and sorter was a young man called Patrick and I was, as usual, Mrs Hawkins, general do-all, proof-reader, literary adviser and secretarial stand-in when the respective secretaries of Mr York and Mr Ullswater left to get married and were never replaced.

2

The Cypriot husband and his English wife in the house next door to Milly's were having a row. It was two in the morning. They had started the rumpus in the garden but had gone indoors to continue it.

Now the first half-flight of Milly's stairs led to a small landing with a window from which you could see straight through the opposite window into the next-door house, three feet away; if you sat on the second half-flight of Milly's stairs you could see the exact equivalent of landing and half-flight next door.

I had been to bed but the fearfulness of the noise on this occasion had brought me down to Milly who was already up in her dressing-gown. The wife next door was screaming. Should we do something? Should we ring the police? We sat on the stairs and watched through the landing windows. Our stair-light was out but theirs was on. Apart from the empty piece of staircase we could see nothing as yet. The rest of our house was quiet, everybody asleep or simply ignoring the noise.

There had been a christening party that afternoon in the house next door. The row concerned the true paternity of the baby boy, some friend of the husband having raised the subject to him, in an aside, at the christening party. I do not think there was any real doubt in the husband's mind that he was the father; only, it gave rationality to the couple's mutual need to dispute, which had spilt rowdily over into the garden; the guests had all gone home.

Evidently, the baby slept through the pandemonium for all we could hear were the wife's shouts and screams and the husband's fury: noises off.

Suddenly they appeared on the stairs, the second half of their staircase, before our eyes, as on a stage. Milly, always with her sense of the appropriate, dashed down to her bedroom and reappeared with a near-full box of chocolates. We sat side by side, eating chocolates, and watching the show. So far, no blows, no fisticuffs; but much waving of arms and menacing. Then the husband seized his wife by the hair and dragged her up a few stairs, she meanwhile beating his body and caterwauling.

Eventually I phoned the police, for the fight was becoming more serious. A policeman arrived at our door within ten minutes. He seemed to take a less urgent view of the din going on in the next-door house and was reluctant to interfere. He joined us on the staircase from where we could now only see the couple's feet as they wrestled. The policeman crowded beside us, for there was no convenient place for him to sit. My hips took up all the spare space. But finally our neighbours descended their staircase so that we could see them in full.

'Can't you stop them?' said Milly, passing the chocolates.

The policeman accepted a chocolate. 'Mustn't come between husband and wife,' he said. 'Inadvisable. You get no thanks, and they both turn on you.'

We could see the force of this argument. Milly offered to make a cup of tea, which she was always ready to do. Finally the policeman said, 'I'll go and have a word with them. This time of night, disturbing the peace.'

We heard him ring their front door-bell; it was a long ring, and at the same time we saw the scene before us disintegrate. The wife and husband sprang apart, she tidying her hair, he pushing his shirt into his trousers. They disappeared from view. From the street came the sound of their front door opening, and the mild reproving voice of the policeman. The wife's voice, thrown high and clear into the empty night, was pleading, apologetic, conciliatory. 'We was just having a bit of an argument, officer.'

The light on the stairs opposite went out. End of the show. Milly and I had a cup of tea in the kitchen and discussed something else.

When I left the house for the office at nine the next morning, the smiling, nut-brown face of our Cypriot neighbour looked up at me from the job he was doing on one of the wheels of his car. 'Good morning, Mrs Hawkins,' he said.

How did he know my name? I didn't know his. People always knew who I was before I knew them, in those days. Later, when I got thin I had to take my chance with everyone else; and this confirms my impression that a great large girl is definitely a somebody, whatever she loses by way of romantic encounters. 'Good morning,' I said.

*

Generally, I got to the office between half-past nine and quarter to ten in the morning. The clock in the big general office was unreliable, and because of a chronic lack of ready cash was likely to remain so. I think that if a clock is not punctual you can't expect the people who live with it to be so. We were all fairly lax about time as the business more and more declined. Patrick, the packer and sorter, was most often the first to arrive, and it was he who would take the first phone calls. I don't know if my memory exaggerates but, looking back, it seems to me that almost every morning I would find Patrick on the phone, shouting to cover his embarrassment and inability to cope with the caller's problem. At that hour the caller was usually an author and the problem was money. Later in the morning, just before noon, the printers and binders would have their hour; their problem too was money, bills unpaid. And certainly, till the bills were paid, there was no hope of sending more books to press.

The telephone: 'Would you mind calling back later? Mrs Hawkins isn't in.' That was Ivy, getting rid of someone. Again, the telephone: 'Ullswater Press,' says Ivy.

Hardly a morning passed but Mabel, the distraught wife of Patrick, would come in to visit him. She invariably turned on me with accusations that I was seducing her husband.

'Mabel! Mabel!' – Patrick was a tall young man with glasses and lanky fair hair, very like a curate in his precocious solemnity; a little younger than me. He was hoping to make a career in publishing; books and reading were his passion. It was true he was attached to me, for he felt he could confide in me. I would listen to him often during the lunch hour when, if it was too cold and rainy to go to the park, we would send out for sandwiches and eat them with our office-made coffee. I think he had married Mabel because she was pregnant. Now Patrick earned very little, but Mabel had a job, and their young child was looked after during the day by Mabel's mother. Whether it was because Patrick was too engrossed in his books to pay attention to his wife or whether he had spoken approvingly of me to her, or whether it was both, Mabel had taken it into her head that I was enticing Patrick away from her. She was in a great state of nerves, and if we had not all tolerated these out-bursts of accusation when she came into our office on her way to work, I think she would have been unable to go on to her job in the offices of a paint firm nearby. As it was, we always calmed her down and she would leave with backward looks of reproach at me on her small blade-like face. 'Mrs Hawkins, you don't know the harm you're doing. Perhaps you don't know,' she said more than once.

'Mabel! Mabel!' said her husband.

Ivy the typist would batter on all through this scene. Cathy the book-keeper, her eyes bulging behind her thick lenses, would rise to her feet, wave her hands, and croak, 'Mrs Hawkins is our editor-in-chief and innocent of the crime.'

Patrick was always mournful after his wife's departure. 'It's good of you to take it like this, Mrs Hawkins,' he would say sometimes, although all I had done was stand in my buxom bulk. And at other times he would say nothing, intensely studying the books he was packing so carefully, so expertly and rapidly.

One of our creditors, a small printer, had taken the diffi-culties of Ullswater Press so personally as to employ a man with a raincoat to stand in the lane outside our office windows all morning and afternoon, staring up. That's all he did: stare up. This was supposed to put us to shame. In the coffee break we did a certain amount of staring back, standing in threes and fours at the window with our cups in our hands. It was strange to see the raincoated man: he was out of place in that smart, expensive area of London; indeed, he was supposed to be shabbily noticeable. In that part of South Kensington from where I emerged every morning from Monday to Friday, the man would have been merely that man-in-the-street that the politicians referred to: one of many. But here in the West End everyone looked at the man, then up at our windows, then back again at him.

At Milly's in South Kensington, everybody paid their weekly rent, however much they had to scrape and budget, balancing the shillings and pence of those days against small fractions saved on groceries and electric light; at Milly's, people added and subtracted, they did division and multiplication sums incessantly; and there was Kate with her good little boxes marked 'bus-fares', 'gas', 'sundries'. Here, in the West End, the basic idea was upper class, scornful of the bothersome creditors as if they were impeding a more expansive view. We, in the noisy general office, were not greatly concerned: after all, the responsibility was not ours, it was that of the Ullswater Press, of Mr Ullswater and of Martin York, and the other names who formed a board of directors; especially of Martin York who ran the firm. It was he who brought me manuscripts he had picked up from his fellow-officers of war-time, or former school friends. 'Will this make a best-seller? Read it and tell me if it might be a best-seller. We need a few best-sellers.' As for the proofs of books waiting to be published, these piled up on my desk, waiting their long turn. I worked on them meticulously; words, phrases, paragraphs, semi-colons. But they remained on my desk long after they were ready to be returned to the printers. New credit from printers and binders was difficult to get. 'Mrs Hawkins, keep those authors away from me.'

Authors – they wanted to know why publication date was always being postponed. The phone would ring. Whereupon Ivy, in her highly affected drawing-room accent, would loudly reply above the auditory effects of our office, 'Mrs Hawkins is in a meeting, I'm afraid. Can I take a message? No, I don't know when she'll be back. No, I can't disturb her, she's in a meeting.' I discovered, after enquiring, that it was an old tradition of the firm, started by Martin York, to say 'in' a meeting, not 'at' a meeting. I supposed 'in' sounded more immersed and not to be disturbed. Ivy had the knack of making 'in a meeting' sound indignant right from the start, as if the very idea of telephoning merely to ask for someone who was thus occupied was an outrage. Ivy had caught the Ullswater Press idea. The floor around Ivy's desk was presently piled with papers, for Mary the filing-clerk left, complaining of the 'atmosphere' created by wild Mabel's visits. Mary was not replaced.

It was after the tea-break that Martin York would usually call down on the intercom. 'Can you spare a minute, Mrs Hawkins?' A minute meant an hour, sometimes more. He wanted to talk, to confide. He would stand at his window looking down at the courtyard at the back of the house and talk. Or he would sit down and talk from the leather armchair opposite mine.

'Sherry? Whisky?' said Martin York.

I accepted a sherry only if he kept me talking after five-thirty, when it was my time to go home. I was used to keeping late office hours, especially now that the office staff was thinning out, and everyone had to take on the jobs of two or more people. In the days when Martin York kept me talking it was a sort of rest. When he spoke of the past, it was the war. When he spoke of the future, it was of the important loan he claimed to have raised to put the firm on its feet. His war exploits were true. As for the loan, I kept in mind a former remark of his: 'If it is widely enough believed that you have money and wealth, Mrs Hawkins, it is the same as having it. The belief itself creates confidence. And confidence, business.' His round face was pock-marked as if he had had smallpox. It was difficult to dislike him; this was not only my feeling but that of all his associates and friends. So that when he put it about from time to time that he had received important backing, if he was not believed, then everybody wanted to believe him, to the effect that he did indeed attract new funds from time to time, and temporarily save the situation.

3

It was when Martin York was especially upset that he would call me up to his office to talk to him. It made me sad to leave the galley-proofs of a novel by Cocteau or a new edition of *Tender is the Night* folded on my desk. Many of the Ullswater Press books were so good, so rare. I enjoyed keeping a sharp eye for typographical errors; I loved to check doubtful points of translations with the greatest care; no matter that the office was a turmoil of mixed sounds and that I was constantly interrupted to answer the telephone or settle some point of contention, I was always happy when checking proofs. '*Evening Dispatch, Evening News*' would come the cry from the newsboy downstairs in the narrow lane; and the telephone would summon me to Mr York's office. On these occasions he gave orders that he wasn't to be disturbed by the telephone or by visitors.

When he was upset he drank whisky. I would talk to him while he sat back in his chair, eyes closed. I never talked about affairs in the office; I spoke of my home life at 14 Church End

Villas, South Kensington. Mr York listened quite intently, as I discovered, for he always remembered some detail of the previous instalments.

'How is Wanda getting on, Mrs Hawkins?'

Wanda, the Polish dressmaker, had enough problems to fill up the rest of the afternoon. Mr York filled his glass, and I him in about Wanda.

'Wanda', I said, 'suffers greatly.'

'I never met a Pole who doesn't.'

'Most of her sufferings derive from her past sufferings. But now she has a new source. It isn't a joke, Mr York. Wanda has a hard life. She has had an anonymous letter.'

Wanda made all my clothes for me. The only other place I could get clothes to fit me at a reasonable price was an Outsize Shop in Oxford Street: these were clothes suitable for everyone, only larger. Wanda, on the other hand, had a flair for divining her clients' personalities. Since she charged me very little, I had to take my chance for an occasional fitting when she wasn't occupied with more profitable clients. This chance often occurred on a Sunday afternoon after five o'clock. Wanda had been to the one-o'clock Polish mass at Brompton Oratory and there, after the service, had met all her friends and relations who were then living in London. Counting the elderly and the children there must have been at least a hundred Polish refugees acquainted with or connected with Wanda. I knew this at first hand because I had accompanied Wanda on a few occasions to the one o'clock Polish mass and national gathering. The Oratory was always crowded. A large number of husbands and fathers were gathered outside the church for the entire service, only turning towards the church doors to sign themselves with the cross at the moment when the bell announced the Elevation.

Wanda was a short plump woman in her late forties. In my memory, it is always winter when Wanda comes to mind on her social occasions outside Brompton Oratory after the Mass. The heavy incense of those days hovered around the doors of the church as the people emerged. Wanda had a thick, shapeless, bristling fur coat of a dark colour, with a fur hat to match. Her pale blonde hair protruded at the back in a thick plaited bun. She had a sweet oval face with small blue eyes. As she talked to her special group of compatriots she would rhythmically bob her whole body forward in emphasis of her words, to the effect that with every bob forward her behind would bob backward as if likewise to emphasize its declarations. The gatherings outside the Oratory which spilled over into Brompton Road would gradually disperse, so gradually that it was not till three in the afternoon that the voluble exiles had moved off, some to visit a nearby museum, the Victoria & Albert or the Natural History, most to crowd into the tea shops where they ate sweet cakes and creamy pastries with tea and lemon. They greatly enriched London with their new and alien life.

As I discovered from Wanda, a good part of the afternoon's conversation consisted in exchanges of émigré survival-lore and items of information about the practical aspects of the country they had come to settle in. Like other groups of war refugees, they brought their courage with them; it was no mean offering. In exchange they visibly and loquaciously went about to discover what funds were available and where. What ministry to apply to? What forms to fill in? What schools, what doctors? And, for the Poles, what Catholic schools and doctors? What organizations, what committees, bursaries, scholarships, what personages, what names, addresses and telephone numbers, and what jobs and what employment agencies? They knew the public libraries, the specialized private libraries and the best reading-rooms. Wanda and her friends certainly knew far more about how to tap the resources of post-war Britain than I did. And it was not all a materialistic process. Some of Wanda's friends were ardent lecture-goers. Word went round about the lectures given in the evenings in London. Someone was always giving a lecture on politics or astronomy, history, Czech poetry, Polish literature, the customs of the Polynesians. I had no idea, until I heard about it from Wanda, that there was so much lecturing going on in London.

In those days of pounds, shillings and pence, Wanda managed on very few of them; her charges for alterations were mostly computed in shillings. Alterations of clothes took up a great many of her working hours; only occasionally did she have to devote her days to an important job – the making of a wedding dress, a coat for the bridegroom's mother or a new summer dress for one of her ladies.

When she didn't have a client being measured or fitted or pinned-up in her room, Wanda continued to work, either by hand or at her sewing-machine, even while her friends and enemies crowded into her room. One of the women would busy herself with tea at the gas-ring while Wanda sewed and talked. She was too busy, herself, to go to lectures and libraries.

The men amongst her Polish friends all looked much older than the women, not old enough to be fathers, but certainly elder brothers. When I accepted one of Wanda's pressing invitations to stay for a refreshment, the conversation was a polite change-over from Polish into English. I got to know and recognize most of Wanda's crowd.

One Saturday morning I had gone down to see if there was any post for me. I passed Wanda on the stairs. She was smiling with her letters in her hand. For me, there was a letter from a cousin. I stood beside the hall-stand, opening it. Suddenly, from Wanda's room came a long, loud, high-pitched cry which diminished into a sustained, distant and still audible ululation.

I ran upstairs. Milly came out to see what was the matter and stood on the lower steps, looking up. I knocked on Wanda's door at the moment that a second lament came piercing from inside the room; I wasted no time in going straight in. There was Wanda in her black working jumper and skirt, her blue carpet-slippers, holding a letter in her hand and the long cry issuing from her mouth. Her eyes were terrorized. She handed me the letter. I made her sit down before I read it, imagining it to be news of a sudden death in the family, at least. The letter read:

Mrs Podolak,

We, the Organisers, have our eyes on you. You are conducting a dressmaking business but you are not declaring your income to the Authorities.

Take care.

An Organiser.

The envelope was cheap brown manilla. It had been posted at Westminster.

'Mrs Hawkins,' said Wanda, 'this is the end of me. They will put me in prison. They will deport me.'

Milly arrived, tapping at the door to see what was the matter. As I let her in, I saw the Carlin couple and Kate Parker, the nurse, standing in their doorways, alarmed. 'It's all right,' I said. 'Wanda's only seen a mouse. Or she thought she did.' Whether they believed me or not I don't know. I pulled Milly inside and shut Wanda's door.

'A lot of rubbish,' said Milly when she had read the letter. 'Who wrote it?'

Wanda cried out that she didn't know such an evil enemy. I said she must keep quiet – 'We don't want the whole house to hear about it.' I wasn't thinking of any danger to Wanda but in fact I judged that the arrival of an anonymous letter would make a bad atmosphere in the house. I hated handling the wretched thing; I had an urge to wash my hands.

'A bit of brandy,' said Milly, who always, in emergency, came straight to the point. She disappeared downstairs, returning with a stiff brandy for Wanda, who was now trembling and whispering that she would go to prison or be deported. 'It is a crime, you don't pay income tax.'

Again, Milly came straight to the point. 'What income?' she said, looking round Wanda's world, her lumpy bed made up in the corner, the pile of old clothes waiting to be altered, with here a pair of men's trousers to be taken in and there someone's dearly treasured small fur collar to be transferred from one coat to another; cotton-reels in a shoe-box, bright scissors on the sewing-table, a little tin box which had once held Allenbury's glycerine and blackcurrant pastilles, and now, Wanda's pins. There was a gas-fire and a gas-ring, the chairs and hanging-cupboard that Milly had acquired second-hand in order to nominally furnish the room; on the mantelpiece was a wood-framed photograph of Wanda's mother and father – the mother standing up, the father sitting, beside a tall vase of flowers – now both dead; a photograph of a Polish soldier with a wide moustache, looking out at his destiny with staring eyes: he had been killed. A picture of a black Madonna, which I now know to be the Madonna of Czestochowa. A photograph of Wanda and her four sisters, one of whom was married in Scotland and the other three of whom were still in Poland and to whom Wanda and her sister sent off parcels of tinned food, warm scarves and stockings every now and then, hoping against hope they would arrive safely. Wanda's suitcases piled dustily on top of the wardrobe. Wanda's sewing-machine was the most expensive thing in the room: Wanda had just finished paying it up. The smell of all this jumble and effort, the smell of bed, of worn clothes, a waft of moth-ball from the strip of fur collar to be transferred, and of soap, of tea and biscuits – this was Wanda's room's special smell, and not at all offensive; I had known it already from my visits to Wanda for the fittings of my clothes and for tea when she held her merry sociable *soirées*. Now there was added the faint smell of brandy, for in her agitation she had spilt some on her jersey.

I remember a lot of sensations clearly from those first moments of Wanda's shock. Part of her brave future was gone forever. I remember her panic-stricken face, her trembling. Nothing Milly or I could suggest would convince her she had nothing to fear. I wanted to take the anonymous letter to the police: she was frantic.

'Look, Wanda,' I said, 'I could fill you out an income-tax form. You have working expenses, you have dependants in Poland; if you let me put down everything clearly you won't have to pay a penny. I'll come with you to the tax-office.'

'Tax-office?' She was breathing heavily. 'Go to the tax-office? They will send me to prison; I go back to Poland.'

Milly kept repeating her dictum that in order to pay income tax you first have to have an income. But this argument only terrorized Wanda the more. She was convinced she would be arrested for coming so late, after all these years. 'I never thought of income tax. How could I think? They will never believe.' The judges, she said, would condemn her. I don't know what picture she had in mind, of how many judges, grand juries, and the clank of prison doors, but she was not to be consoled. Plainly, she had come from a world of bureau-cratic tyranny infinitely worse than ours. In a way, I felt she wanted to embrace this suffering; she was conditioned to it.

What I wanted to know was who had sent the letter. That was the question working and lurking in my mind all the time we were trying to convince Wanda she had nothing to fear. It seemed to me vastly more important to locate the anonymous fiend than to bother about Wanda's tax return. Who was this 'Organiser'? This was in Milly's mind, too.

'No, no,' said Wanda, 'none of my friends, my worst enemy, nobody from Poland could do such a thing. How could they do it?'

'It must be someone who knows you, who knows a little about you, Wanda.'

'Someone in this house,' said Wanda.

'Never,' said Milly. 'It must be one of your customers or those friends and cousins.'

'Why should they?' Wanda said, and wailed, with her hands over her eyes. I was sure that Wanda would think of a possible someone after she had calmed down.

Milly was now anxious. I spent Saturday afternoon discussing it with her. Wanda had taken a sleeping pill and gone to bed, and we had promised to keep all of her visitors away with the excuse that she had been obliged to go out to the suburbs to measure a new lady, very important. Wanda had let me take the letter away with me. I wanted to study it.

'The swine!' said Milly. She was certain it was a man who had written the letter. 'It could never be a woman,' said Milly, when I raised that possibility. I inclined to agree with her but I couldn't think of a respectable reason for eliminating a female suspect.

Although Milly wasn't prepared to admit to Wanda the possibility that someone in the house, or connected with the house, had written the letter, she was ready to discuss the eventuality with me, if only for the purpose of eliminating it. Who were 'the organisers' and who the 'organiser' who had written the letter?

It was written on blue Basildon Bond paper in smallish writing, near to what used to be known as 'script', an adaptation of ordinary book-print to cursive handwriting. It looked as if this was the writer's normal hand, but here and there obviously disguised, so that some of the 'd's were larger than the natural proportions of the rest; the word 'business' sloped to the right, with the effect of italics; and some of the individual letters were slanted, too, although the writing in general was upright. I looked at the letter with half-closed eyes, to get a sense of it. For an instant I thought I recognized it, without being able to place it. But when I opened my eyes to study it closer, the sensation had gone. Certainly I wasn't able to recognize any handwriting in the context of Wanda, the house, or Wanda's acquaintance. I suppose I had noticed letters addressed to her lying on the hall table or on the mat inside the front door, but I had never taken any particular notice of the writing. As for the other occupants of the house, I had never seen their handwriting apart from Milly's which was something of a scrawl. But what struck me was the difference between the benighted tone of the letter and the relatively educated hand; it seemed a deliberate literary performance of poor quality, an attempt at parody, if a lame one. Someone had invented the 'Organisers' in order to scare Wanda. If she had belonged to my own world, that of books and publishing, I would perhaps have known where to begin in sorting out the vaguely possible culprits; I say 'vaguely possible' because even among the people I knew and came up against in my working life, some of whom included the more viperish and base examples of literary hackdom, I would have been hard put to it to select any one. But to try to discern any shape or form in Wanda's ambience was absolutely to flounder in a fog.

Milly was upset at the suggestion that it was someone in the house, to the point of being almost mesmerized by the idea. She also feared further letters. 'These things happen in threes,' said Milly in her way of uttering bits of folk-wisdom; she was spooning tea into the heated teapot. She always mixed tea with maxims.

We decided to go through the occupants of the house, one by one.

Basil and Eva Carlin, in their large bed-sitting-room and small kitchen on the first floor: 'I can't see them doing it,' I said.

'Neither can I,' said Milly. 'They're so quiet. Never a murmur and the rent paid on the dot.'

'It's often the quiet types who do these things,' I said.

'That's very true. You've got a point, there.'

'What exactly does he do?'

'Well,' said Milly, 'I only know he's got a job with an engineering firm at Clapham, keeping the books.'

One of the few occasions that I had exchanged a few words with Basil Carlin was when we found each other on the top deck of the same bus, and the only vacant seat was next to me. That was when he told me he was an 'engineering accountant'. A quiet type, yes, but not creepy. I hated having to think of these normal neighbours of mine, whom I passed on the stairs, as suspects. I thought of Eva, respectfully sidling through Milly's kitchen in the afternoon to hang out her husband's shirts to dry in the back garden. She was a thin and wispy woman who had a habit of walking with her elbows out. Basil was of medium height and build with thin fair hair and glasses. There was nothing wrong with them, nothing at all.

'It's awful,' said Milly, 'to have to go through them all one by one like this.'

'I was thinking the same thing. I feel treacherous.'

It was true that the search for the offender put us in a sense on the same debased level. But I was determined to exhaust every possibility as impartially as possible. I would much have preferred to take the letter to the police.

'What could the Carlins have against Wanda?' Milly said. 'They've never had words with anyone in the house. Wanda let down a hem for her the other day.'

'Oh, she let down a hem for her?'

All right, she let down a hem for Eva Carlin. I said, 'Do you know what their handwriting's like?'

'Never seen it. They pay in cash.' We all paid in cash. The less you put on paper the better, was one of Milly's opinions.

Wanda let down a hem for Eva Carlin. That's all we know. I turned to plump Kate Parker with her white, bright teeth, the vigorous cockney cleaning her room, even now, upstairs, on a Saturday afternoon. We could hear the furniture being moved out on the landing in the process of her war against germs. I thought of her boxes marked 'electricity', 'gas', 'bus-fares', 'sundries'. Everything organized.

'Not Kate,' said Milly. 'That I could never believe.'

Nor could I. In spite of the fact that Kate disapproved of Wanda's over-stuffed room and crowded alien lifestyle, I couldn't believe it of Kate.

But Kate was an organizer by nature. I wondered how she spelt the word 'organizer', which in the letter was spelt with an 's'.

I took Wanda up a cup of tea at about five o'clock. She was awake and crying. She had got right into bed and unloosed her hair. It was the first time I had seen her with this quantity of natural corn-coloured hair about her face and shoulders. She made a very impressive sight. It occurred to me she might well have a lover, or at least an admirer, someone who courted her and who had a rival, a rejected vindictive somebody, or a jealous woman whose man Wanda had attracted. Perhaps we don't observe each other well enough, I thought. Seeing Wanda in this new light, not only a worthy Polish matron, but a sex-potential, I could see that the range of suspects was vastly increased. But I didn't like to say, right away, 'Wanda, do you know of any man, woman, who could be sentimentally roused for you, against you?' – I didn't say this because at that moment she would certainly have exploded with indignation. The image she showed to the world was that of a church-going seamstress and dedicated widow. And indeed I didn't see where she would have found time to fit in a love-affair, nor the hint of a flirtation.

Anyway, she was crying and lamenting so much that any form of rational enquiry was useless. Oh God! She might milk this event for the rest of her life. 'Wanda,' I said, 'you have to ignore it. If there are any more we'll take them to the police.'

'Any more? Any more? . . . The police!'

Milly opened the door and came in. I could see, as she looked at blue-eyed Wanda for the first time sitting up in bed with her fair hair flowing around her, that the same thought struck her as had struck me: Wanda was an attractive woman, Wanda was sexy. It was something which, stupidly, we hadn't thought of before.

'I have enemies,' wailed Wanda.

'Leave them to God,' said Milly.

We left Wanda to her tea. 'But', said Milly, 'she often spoke of her friends and her enemies. Now she's surprised she has enemies. She always said "my friends and my enemies", as if they were to be expected. Foreigners always talk like that, mind you. And when you think of the number of people that come to this door for Wanda . . .'

'She looks pretty with her hair down,' I said.

'Doesn't she, now?' said Milly.

That evening, after supper, we went through the possibilities of the other tenants in the house. There was my neighbour on the top floor, young Isobel, who had such a lot of friends and who rang her Daddy every evening. Here again, Milly and I blinked at each other. Isobel, of all people to write a nasty anonymous letter . . . 'I've met her father,' said Milly, as if that settled the question. I hadn't met him, myself, but it was true that the presence of Isobel's father's voice in her daily life seemed to give her a sort of stability; but even more than those telephone calls to her father, it was rather her vivacity and her silly crowd of young friends that put Isobel out of the question. Surely no one as careless and carefree as Isobel, as she ran out of the house into the waiting taxis or the boyfriend's car, could have written that mean letter? It was someone broody, with inner malice, whom we were looking for.

Milly felt as guilty in her way as I did in mine as we sat discussing and analysing the people who shared the same house with us. I noticed that, although we always came to the same conclusions, Milly's reasons were different from mine: she tended to exonerate all tenants of hers because they were her tenants, while I took a more objective look at them. I felt it came to the same thing, for Milly had already done her sizing-up when she took the people under her roof. Still, we could be mistaken. And we felt obscurely guilty. The letter, lying on Milly's table, was a thing of guilt, arising from guilt, causing it.

There remained William Todd, the student in his final year of medicine. I say he remained, although in fact from a strictly impartial point of view the suspects in the house would have included both Milly and me. I pointed this out to Milly, who said, 'Whatever would you and I do a thing like that for?' I felt, then, that this was the real question to be asked of all of us. What would be the point in any one of us molesting Wanda? Why? What for? William Todd's wireless programme was going on upstairs, sifting down to us as we were talking. He was usually out on a Saturday evening, but tonight he was studying. Generally, in the evenings he thumped down the stairs with his sturdy legs and went out to meet his friends at the coffee bar near South Kensington station. I had seen him there several times if I happened to be returning home late, myself. He would be with a group of young men and women who looked like the fellow students that they were. Why on earth should William take it into his head to write a scurrilous, anonymous letter to Wanda? He probably didn't ever think of her unless he happened to pass her on the stair.

'So it's none of us,' said Milly. 'It must be one of Wanda's people, from outside. And I'm going to tell her so in the morning.' As the evening proceeded, Wanda became almost herself a culprit in our minds: she was guilty of being a victim of the guilty missive lying on Milly's table, author unknown, exuding malignity all over the kitchen.

4

'Wanda looks out of the window,' I told Martin York. 'She sees spies standing at the corner of the road. She sees spies in the grocer shop, following her. Private detectives and government spies.'

Wanda's troubles were now known throughout 14 Church End Villas, South Kensington. She was unable to keep it a secret at the same time as she lamented that everyone was talking about her. Even the people at No. 16, the Cypriot and his English wife, were by some means thoroughly informed of the affair before the week was out. They even called to express their solidarity, the husband earnestly offering to break the neck of the offender should we ever be in a position to name him or her or them. 'They call themselves "Organisers",' I said, hoping it might mean something to the couple.

'Organizers!' said the wife. 'I'll organize them, just let me get my hands on them.'

Mr Twinny, the odd-job man who lived at No. 30, was equally indignant. 'No gentleman', he told me in a hushed, confiding tone, 'would ever do such a thing to a lady. A widow at that.'

Wanda was now in difficulties with her work. Her clients were puzzled at her sullen fearfulness; they came for their fittings and asked Milly on the way out, had they done anything to offend?

'Wanda's not herself just now,' Milly would say.

'What's happened? What's the matter?'

'It'll pass, mark my words,' Milly always said.

But her Polish friends were not to be put off. Within a fortnight they had all got to hear of her anonymous letter; within another fortnight they came asking Wanda to be reasonable and shake off the shock – 'After all, what can they do to you? . . . After all, there is no threat and extortion . . . After all, it is some crazy person, he sends out this letter by the hundreds, the thousands, this person.'

When I described the letter to Martin York I was impressed by his spontaneous generosity in offering the services of his own lawyer, at his own expense, to help Wanda. He was genuinely outraged at the story. At that time Martin York was himself more deeply in trouble than I knew. Some months later, when the judge at his trial told how 'Commercial life cannot be carried on unless people are honest,' and sentenced him to seven years, I remembered his simple gesture to Wanda, an obscure immigrant seamstress in South Kensington whom he had only heard of through me.

At the same time Martin York was full of unconventional advice which savoured of officers'-mess lore. 'The way to throw the income tax, Mrs Hawkins,' he said, 'is to send them, out of the blue, a cheque for eight pounds seventeen and three. Something like that. They can never tally up a sum of that kind with any of their figures; your file goes from hand to hand for months and years, and eventually gets lost.'

'I wouldn't like to try it,' I said. 'It would be one's money that would get lost.'

'I daresay, Mrs Hawkins.'

I took things more or less literally in those days; perhaps that was why he felt I was reliable and safe.

In the event Wanda didn't consult the lawyer about the letter; she was too terrified. But eventually she let the Ullswater Press accountant put her income tax right. She owed a little over twelve pounds, of which, some months later, she got a rebate of four. For the time being there was no further anonymous letter, and generally the first high tide of horror, puzzlement and suspicion died down in the house. It died down but it didn't quite die. I would find myself looking strangely at one of the tenants or at one of Wanda's visitors; I would wonder. And since I wondered and even sometimes pondered, I supposed that the other tenants did more or less the same. They must have thought, they must have speculated. I know that Milly was vigilant about everyone who came to the door for Wanda. 'A lady for a fitting,' she would report; 'the old priest; her young cousin that's going to be a priest; that fellow from the Post Office with a suit to be altered; that Polish family that bring her those cakes; those two Polish sisters that teach music . . .'

But I was more active in my investigations. It is amazing what one progressively learns about people through an attempt to dispel suspicion. I went about it by simply getting more friendly with each one of them.

Then, Wanda herself was far more subdued than she had ever been before. She slowed down; she seemed to age and begin to fade. Time would have done these things for her anyway, as for us all. But then and there, for Wanda, it was the work of the anonymous letter-writer, the infamous 'Organiser'. Wanda had left the letter in my hands, for I promised her I would continue to investigate and try and find who her enemy was. I felt that samples of handwriting were things to get hold of as unnoticeably as possible. I bought a book about handwriting, and I remember going over the letter, alone in my room, night after night, studying the formation of the letters through a magnifying glass. I am a neat note-taker: I bought a quarto-sized notebook and began to make notes of the graphological features of the letter – looped 'l's and unlooped 'h's, closed 'o's and unclosed 'a's, 'f's exaggerated in such a way as to suggest a fake. For the letter yielded all the symptoms of a disguised hand, that is, small inconsistencies, like the contradictions of a guilty person under interrogation. Above all, I was looking for the organizer spelt with an 's'. I tried collecting as many examples of handwriting with words ending in 'ize' as I could. But in most cases – for instance 'realize' and 'recognize' where the alternative spellings 'realise' or 'recognise' are common – one could draw no conclusion.

But there was some element in Wanda's life, I was sure, which held the clue; it was perhaps something of which Wanda herself was unaware, or some person she had completely forgotten.

In the meantime she mourned, no longer so much for her own potential plight in the hands of the Inland Revenue department but on the much more reasonable grounds that someone she had known was gratuitously vicious.

'Good morning, Mrs Hawkins.' This was the Cypriot next door cleaning his bicycle as I left for the office. 'Good morning, Marky.' That was the name he demanded to go by; he was decidedly embarrassed when any of us made to call him Mr something. It was to be a while before I found myself being addressed by my first name. This certainly coincided with the time when I was moved to lose my great weight. Then, I invited people to call me Nancy, instead of Mrs Hawkins as I was to everyone in that summer of 1954, when I went to my office in the morning partly by bus and partly across Green Park, whether it rained or whether it didn't.

Suicide is something we know too little about, simply because the chief witness has died, frequently with his secret that no suicide-note seems adequate to square with the proportions of the event. But what we call suicidal action, an impetuous career towards disaster that does not necessarily end in the death of the wild runner, was going on at the Ullswater Press. That spring I had reason to reflect on Martin York's precipitous course towards a heavy reckoning when I heard on the wireless – it was May 6th – that the runner, Roger Bannister, had beaten the world record: a mile in under four minutes. Martin York, I reflected, was going faster than that, he was going at something like a mile a minute, even when he sat hemmed-in, drinking whisky. One day he called me to his office. He was signing some documents. 'Will you witness these signatures, Mrs Hawkins?' I poised my pen and drew towards me the papers he had already signed, while he signed one further document. But I didn't sign my name: I saw they were letters to banks and I saw that the signatures, although they were in Martin York's natural writing, were not his. And I saw that one of the signatures was 'Arthur Cary'. Sir Arthur Cary was in those days the top financier, always in the news with his larky wife. I had no time to see anything else. Martin York, foreseeing my objection, had snatched back the documents.

'You aren't forging signatures are you, Mr York?' I said in a joking way, not absolutely to offend.

'Forging? Of course not. Forging is copying someone else's signature. Arthur told me I could write his name, it's all right. But I see there's no need to get the signatures witnessed.' Martin York put the papers in a drawer.

Many months later I knew that what I had seen was part of a fraudulent act so naive that it was bound to be discovered. At the time I decided it couldn't possibly be a serious fraudulent act simply because it was so naive. I thought at the time that it was one of Martin York's bits of self-irony on his suicidal career to business ruin. For ruin was certainly ahead. He had that year taken on a few 'literary advisers', mostly young men of good family and no brains whose fathers had pleaded them a job. They were on the payroll. They amused us when they came into the office, which was usually on Friday, the pay day. They lasted for three or four weeks, and replaced each other in quick succession. The reason why their terms of office were so short was that Mr Ullswater would remonstrate with Martin York: 'Who was that young man I saw downstairs?' or 'Who is that insufferable youth making scented tea in the general office?' Martin York would explain to the effect that the young man was learning the business. But so frequently did they find no paypacket waiting for them that they drifted away, much to the typist Ivy's regret.

But more serious for the failing firm were the hangers-on who now got round Martin York to agree to publish their frightful books.

Sometimes, I think, his desire to sign up these books for his publishing house was not due to a lack of discrimination so much as to the common fallacy which assumes that if a person is a good, vivacious talker he is bound to be a good writer. This is by no means the case. But Martin York had another, special illusion: he felt that men or women of upper-class background and education were bound to have advantages of talent over writers of modest origins. In 1954 quite a few bright publishers secretly believed this.

Publishers, for obvious reasons, attempt to make friends with their authors; Martin York tried to make authors of his friends. He promised contracts to the most talkative, gossipy, amusing members of his own class, his old schoolfellows, their wives, his former army companions and their wives.

This was where I had to intervene. It often fell to me to turn down a book for which Martin York, during a drinking session, had offered a contract, without even looking at the work. His friends would know where Martin York spent his after-office hours, between six and nine. They went there shamelessly to listen to his woes, and although everyone in the publishing and literary worlds knew that the Ullswater Press was falling to bits, the flocks of carrion crow descended on Martin for the last-minute pickings. I had to shoo them off the next day.

At this point the man whom I came to call the *pisseur de copie* enters my story. I forget which of the French symbolist writers of the late nineteenth century denounced a hack writer as a urinator of journalistic copy in the phrase '*pisseur de copie*', but the description remained in my mind, and I attached it to a great many of the writers who hung around or wanted to meet Martin York; and finally I attached it for life to one man alone, Hector Bartlett.

The term 'upper class' in those days meant more than it does now. Hector Bartlett claimed at every opportunity, both directly and by implication, to be upper class, to the effect that I presumed him to be rather low-born; in fact, I was right, and I wasn't alone in my suppositions. But a great many people fell in with Hector's pretensions, a surprising number, especially those simple souls who quell their doubts because they cannot bring themselves to discern a blatant pose; the effort would be too wearing and wearying, and might call for an open challenge, and lead to unpleasantness.

He used to waylay me in Green Park on my way to work or on my way home. Occasionally this amused me, for I might egg him on to show off his social superiority, and, not less, the superior learning that he claimed. For he knew the titles of all the right books, and the names of the authors, but it amounted to nothing; he had read very little.

What he wanted from me was an introduction to Martin York and through him to his uncle, a film producer.

Pisseur de copie! Hector Bartlett, it seemed to me, vomited literary matter, he urinated and sweated, he excreted it.

'Mrs Hawkins, I take incalculable pains with my prose style.'

He did indeed. The pains showed. His writings writhed and ached with twists and turns and tergiversations, inept words, fanciful repetitions, far-fetched verbosity and long, Latin-based words.

I became aware one morning that his meeting me in Green Park on my way to the office was not by chance. He had met me once too often. It was a clear day in June, and that it was a Monday I know from the fact that I was thinking with a happiness, new to me for many years, of young Isobel's Daddy to whom she telephoned from her room in our house every night, and whom I had met, in church, the day before. It was an Anglo-Catholic church in Queen's Gate. As I stood for the 'Kyrie Eleison' I noticed Isobel with an older man two rows in front. I assumed it was her father and so it proved to be when we came out of church and Isobel introduced him. Hugh Lederer. I had thought for the first time for the many years of my widowhood, when I had seen him with Isobel to the sweet music of the 'Kyrie': there's an attractive man. And now, crossing Green Park on this fresh Monday morning in June, the 'Kyrie' sang in my head, and the meeting in church, and the unpremeditated lunch to follow, and the rest of the sweet Sunday afternoon retold itself to my mind. It was no pleasure at all to see Hector Bartlett hovering in my path, I didn't feel in the mood to humour him that morning. He had seen me approaching before I had seen him, and now he stood by a bench affecting to wonder whether to sit down on it. He stood there, at nine-fifteen in the morning, the last person I wanted to enter into my sensations just then, but emphatically determined to do so. Red hair *en brosse*, brown corduroy trousers, tweed coat with leather patches on the sleeves, a yellow tie and a green check shirt: this was gaudy for those days, and Hector Bartlett was always dressed in bright colours. He was tall, with a pronounced stoop of the shoulders which made him seem older than he was – I imagine, at that time, he would be in his mid-thirties. His face was round with a second fat chin. He had a small but full baby-mouth as if forever asking to suck a dummy tit.

On the path, walking in front of me, was a young couple with their arms affectionately round each other's waists. They blocked Hector, the *pisseur de copie*, from my view. They looked as if they were on their way to work, probably in the same office, for this was the hour of the office-workers. When they passed the park-bench around which Hector Bartlett had been hovering I saw that he had sat down; he was waiting for me, and now rose to meet me.

'Good morning, Mrs Hawkins, what a pleasant surprise!' He indicated the two lovers who had passed. 'Dalliance!' he said.

I don't know what got into me, for I said, not to myself as usual, but out loud, '*Pisseur de copie!*'

'What was that, Mrs Hawkins?' He looked dismayed, then incredulous, and finally he decided not to believe his ears. He didn't wait for me to answer or explain but gave a little joyless laugh and said, 'Beautiful morning.'

'Aren't you working to-day?' I said.

I forget what he replied. He had no regular job that I was aware of. He sometimes reviewed books in provincial papers and lived mostly on his wits and a novelist called Emma Loy. But I had nothing against him on that score. I knew a great many obscure writers, it is true mostly younger than Hector

45

Bartlett, who had to scrub around for a living and share their casual earnings with a partner, or who lived on other writers more fortunate than themselves. And as for Hector Bartlett, I had once, some years before, put him in the way of a job that would have suited him very well: door-to-door encyclopaedia-pushing in the suburbs. He would have been able to blab and enthuse about the encyclopaedias, and impress the house-wives. But he turned down the job, as he had every right to do. What I found so frightful about him was that he was always trying to use me, or further some scheme of his through my presumed influence with Martin York.

That morning, he walked with me as far as the office door, pressing on me an idea he had to turn a novel into a film. Martin York's uncle was a film producer, a very rich man, all of whose riches however could not, in the end, save Martin York from gaol. At the moment this was not to be foreseen, and Hector Bartlett was spoiling my fresh June morning with his unwanted company, aggravating the situation by starting to describe the novel which he wanted to adapt.

'I know the novel,' I said.

It was one of Emma Loy's novels. She was then already in her forties, a well-known writer. Hector Bartlett had recently established himself as her hanger-on. Wherever she went these days he had to go. It was a phenomenon nobody could explain. Emma Loy was a beautiful writer, and had enough sense to know that he was not. Yet she tried to get him published by all the magazines and publishers who wanted her work. She introduced him to everyone she knew who might be influential and they, amazed, did nothing for him whatsoever.

Emma Loy was a striking woman with a strong face and light brown hair combed back off her face. She always wore grey, and it suited her. I had known her for some time. I don't know what had got into her head when she took up Hector Bartlett. It probably flattered her to have a man nearly ten years her junior in constant attention. I don't believe she was in love with him. How could she have been? She was a sensible and imaginative woman, she had wit, on some occasions magic. Later, when it became too embarrassing for her to carry her world-wide reputation, a new and real man in her life, and the *pisseur* as well, she wriggled out of the relationship. But she had to pay for it.

That time had not yet come and here was Hector Bartlett with her permission to make a film-script out of her novel.

'I have the exclusive rights from Emma,' he said. 'It's a must for S. T. York.'

'Then write to S. T. York,' I said.

'It would be preferable to procure an introduction from Martin York,' he said. 'It would be let us say a decided feather in Martin's cap. You yourself should have a word in Martin's ear with regard to the possibility of transmuting this fine work of fiction to a saga of the silver screen. Nepotism is still I believe the order of the day.'

How could Emma Loy stand him? We got as far as the office door. It was just before nine-thirty. He wanted to come upstairs with me and continue his 'talk about the film-script'.

'I'm afraid it isn't convenient. Good-bye, Mr Bartlett.'

'Won't you call me Hector?'

To my own astonishment I said, 'No, I call you *Pisseur de copie*.'

The morning noise of the office took over. I remember it now in these sweet waking hours of the night that I still treasure so much, here far away from the scene of my life in those days, far away in time.

The morning clattered on, with the sound of Ivy's typewriter and Cathy the book-keeper's muttering, the sound of all our shoes on the bare boards of the office floor and the rattle of cups as one of us made the tea. There was also the usual visit of Patrick's wife, Mabel, who that morning had found someone other than me to make a scene about, and whose noise-creating was indirect, consisting of the efforts of the others to reason her out of her fit. The outside telephone shrilled and the intercom buzzed. Ivy responded superciliously.

'Mr York is in a meeting. May I take a message?' – 'Mr Ullswater is out of London for a few days. Who is calling? Can you spell that name, please?' (Ivy's 'n's sounded 'd' so that 'name' sounded like 'dame') – 'Mrs Hawkins is in a meeting. Oh, I don't know when she'll be free, would you like to try again?' – 'I'm afraid that Mrs Hawkins . . .'

Out of this general din, I heard my name wanted on the phone rather more frequently than usual.

'Who are the people on the phone for me, Ivy?' I said.

'It's one lady only. A Mrs Emma Loy. She'll ring again, it's urgent.'

Everyone who rang our office was always urgent, but Emma Loy was important even though she didn't publish her books with the likes of us. I told Ivy, 'Next time she rings I'll take the call.'

She rang on the stroke of twelve. I remember this fact because it was my habit to silently recite the Angelus at twelve noon, and even if I was interrupted in the middle of it, the phrases went on in my head.

The angel of the Lord brought the tidings to Mary . . .

'It's Mrs Loy for you, Mrs Hawkins,' Ivy sang out.

And she conceived by the Holy Ghost . . .

'Hallo, Mrs Loy. How are you?'

'I'm very worried. About Hector. What exactly did you do to him this morning?'

'Me? Nothing. He wants to make a film out of one of your novels.'

Hail Mary, full of grace, the Lord . . .

'He said you called him something, some very, very, strange epithet.'

. . . is with thee, blessed art thou . . .

'All I said was "*pisseur de copie*". It's the absolute truth. Now, isn't it?'

She must have known that it was. 'Mrs Hawkins!' she said, and rang off.

And the Word was made flesh . . .

That day I lost my job with the Ullswater Press. Martin York was in tears when he told me I had to go. Emma Loy had powerful friends in publishing and printing and, even worse, in the whisky business that Martin York was desperately trying to retrieve his fortunes by.

'Why did you say it? What made you? It was a disastrous thing to say to anyone, Mrs Hawkins, especially to a close friend, and such a close friend, of Emma Loy.'

The late afternoon sun touched lovingly on the rooftops reminding me of time past and time to come, making light of the moment. I had really wanted to go. Really, I had. 'I'll send you your paypacket,' said Martin York in a broken voice. And I wasn't in the least surprised that he didn't.

He was tried in October on eight charges of uttering forged bankers' documents and intent to defraud. The case was all over the papers. Martin York pleaded guilty and was sentenced to seven years' imprisonment, a stiff term even for those days. 'Commercial life', said the judge, 'cannot be carried on unless people are honest'; which simple sentiment was almost word for word what I had once told him myself. Only, I wouldn't have jailed him for seven years on the strength of it.

After the sentence Hector Bartlett wrote numerous gloating articles about Martin York, full of vindictive and invented anecdotes which implied a close acquaintance. They appeared in some of the popular papers and got lost with the rest of the newspaper pulp. It wasn't till many years later that the *Pisseur* himself resurrected them, added to and embroidered them, in his ridiculous old-age memoirs printed at his own expense, subtitled *Farewell, Leicester Square.* I read them only a few years ago, having picked up the book quite by chance on a remainder bookstall.

5

I had some savings and a small pension, so I had no need to find another job immediately. In the months between my abrupt departure from the Ullswater Press and Martin York's arrest I wasted my time with a sense of justified guilt. I enjoy a puritanical and moralistic nature; it is my happy element to judge between right and wrong, regardless of what I might actually do. At the same time, the wreaking of vengeance and imposing of justice on others and myself are not at all in my line. It is enough for me to discriminate mentally and leave the rest to God.

'Commercial life cannot be carried on unless people are honest.' But no life can be carried on satisfactorily unless people are honest. About the time that the Ullswater Press folded up I recall reading a book about one of the martyred Elizabethan recusant priests. The author wrote, 'He was accused of lying, stealing and even immorality.' I noted the quaint statement because although by immorality he meant extramarital sex as many people do, I had always thought that lying and stealing, no less, constituted immorality.

In those months before his arrest Martin York telephoned me, at first frequently. He needed someone to whom to say 'I must restore confidence in the business. Credibility, Mrs Hawkins. I must find other avenues. If I might say so without exaggeration I have a first-rate brain, some say brilliant.'

To answer the telephone in Milly's house one had to stand in the hallway. There was no chair. It was not a suitable place for long conversations, especially with my great weight on my legs. I felt uncomfortable in every way, now, talking to him. It is not because we are rats that we tend to abandon people who are down, it is because we are embarrassed.

'What good has he ever done you?' Milly said. 'Giving you the sack on the spot after all your work and overtime, and owing you your pay.' He stopped telephoning after a while, perhaps not insensitive to my discomfort. But in the first weeks of my idleness I was incessantly called to the phone by the rest of the office about books in production left lying where I had left off, and the panic of their knowing that no one was coming to replace me. Cathy the book-keeper rang me.

'You have to realize', I said, 'that the firm is broke. It's only a matter of time. Why don't you all look for another job?'

'Another job I never find,' Cathy said. 'Where is another job for me? I know exclusively the Ullswater Press. Without the job I put my head in the gas oven.'

This was something I felt she would never do. It is true that survivors from the death-camps had been known to inflict on themselves later in life the very death they had escaped, but these were few. Cathy's experience had made of her a natural survivor. Besides, I reflected, no one seriously talks of suicide in a special form unless they have envisaged it; in Cathy's case

I knew she had no gas stove. The room in Golders Green where she lived was one of ten in a converted house; each was equally fitted with an electric fire, an electric hot-plate and a meter. There was no housekeeper's flat: Cathy paid her rent to an agency. I had been to supper with Cathy. She cooked on a many-tiered type of pot on the *bain-marie* principle, the lower pot being filled with water and gradually heating the others. From this contraption she had produced an impressive meal. But there was no gas-oven, no gas at all in the house, a fact that Cathy lamented. I promised to let her know if I heard of a job suitable for her. There was small hope that anyone would employ Cathy.

'A job in publishing,' specified Cathy with determination.

'Why?' I said.

'I don't want to come down in life,' said this brave woman.

It was likewise with the rest of the staff of the Ullswater Press. Ivy, whose total office experience was less than eighteen months, told me, 'I look up the wanted secretarial in the papers every day but there's nothing in publishing, Mrs Hawkins.'

Mabel, Patrick's fraught wife, telephoned me.

'Mrs Hawkins, is it true that the Press is busting up?'

'I think so, Mabel,' I said severely, not wishing her to over-look and forget her jealous scenes in the office.

'And what is Patrick going to do, may I ask?'

'You may ask,' I said. 'But ask Patrick, not me.'

'But he has to have a job with books. He's writing a book, Mrs Hawkins.'

'Well, tell him to try a book warehouse or a bookshop. I'm afraid I have to go, I've got something on the stove.'

It was a relief one evening to be called to the phone, not the one in the hall but young Isobel's private phone. She knocked at my door. 'I've got Daddy on the line, Mrs Hawkins. He wants to speak to you.' He wanted to ask me to dinner at the Savoy next Saturday, and I accepted with pleasure and joy. He said, 'I look forward to that very much, Mrs Hawkins. I'll pick you up at seven-thirty, all right?'

'Seven-thirty, Mr Lederer.'

I, too, looked forward to that very much. I sat chatting for a while in Isobel's neat attic room, and would have chatted on had her telephone not begun to squeal again; some boyfriend or other.

Isobel was fair in colouring. The father was grey-haired, not old. I would have liked to know more about him, but I left Isobel to her phone calls. When we had all had lunch together after church the previous Sunday we hadn't touched on anything so private as his wife, whether she was at home, dead or divorced. This was, in theory, something I should have known before accepting a dinner date with him. But only in theory. Nobody except mad Mabel would have put me in the husband-snatching class: I was Mrs Hawkins. I put my mind to what I would wear. For special occasions I had my black lace dress and my fur cape. I busied myself with shaking out the fur and pressing the dress. It was five years old but I didn't want to dip into my good nest-egg for a new party dress in haste, and with all the difficulties of my size, simply on the strength of dinner at the Savoy.

'He must be well-to-do, Mrs Hawkins,' said Milly. 'See how he provides for Isobel, her phone and her toll-calls every day, and look at her clothes. She takes a taxi when she wants.'

'Where's the wife?' I said.

'I'll find out from Isobel,' Milly said.

I begged her not to question Isobel just at this time. Isobel would know exactly why she was being questioned.

Milly said, 'When I met him I thought he was a lovely gentleman. He would do lovely for you, Mrs Hawkins.'

'I can't forget the past,' I said, for I had loved my late husband most dearly. I said, 'It could never be quite the same.' But in cases like this, we never want it to be quite the same.

That week I was called downstairs to the phone by Emma Loy.

'Yes, Mrs Loy?'

'Oh, Mrs Hawkins, I just wanted you to know that I've no ill-feelings. I understand you left Ullswater Press, am I right?'

'Yes, I lost my job.'

'I want you to know that I wouldn't, myself, dream of giving Hector an introduction to Martin York's uncle. Hector is not to be trusted. As for the film of any of my novels, I've no need whatsoever for introductions. I'm not even sure that Hector is quite the person to adapt them. It was only that I thought it strange, the objection coming from you, and Hector was offended. I had to say a word.'

'He is a *pisseur de copie*,' I said.

'Jobs in publishing, Mrs Hawkins, are very hard to come by. You might bear that in mind. I could put in a word for you in many quarters. Only you must, simply must, retract.'

'I've got something boiling over, Mrs Loy.'

Saturday night, there I sat at the Savoy, by candlelight, eating their speciality of salmon mousse and sipping white wine, opposite Hugh Lederer, feeling quite as well turned-out as anyone else in the room.

I forget what we ordered next: something exotic. This was

55

in the last few weeks of all food-rationing and the Savoy was making an anticipatory splash. But I ate very little of the exotic dish because it was at this point that Hugh Lederer leaned forward and put his hand on mine. 'Mrs Hawkins,' he said, with a change of voice.

He had a good voice, full of deep modulations. In appearance – and I try to see him as I had seen him so far – he was very well built, not fat, but large and slightly taller than me. He had that sort of tanned and lined face I had always associated with retired civil servants from the Colonies and with secretaries of golf clubs.

'Mrs Hawkins,' he said, 'I can see you are a very understanding woman.'

I didn't care greatly for this; I thought the gesture came too soon and the words made me out to be some kind of a comforter, if not an outright madam. I said absolutely nothing and he took his hand away. I felt rather sorry for him, then, and supposed he was only a bit awkward. During the mousse he had told me he was in the porcelain business and had plans for opening up a trading line in Czechoslovakia and Bavaria. I had told him in return that I liked fine china and admired old Czechoslovakian glass.

I hadn't had time to tell him I had lost my job. Only the Sunday before, when I had lunch with him and Isobel after church, I had been saying how interesting it was to work in publishing.

He said, now, 'I wonder if my daughter Isobel would do well in publishing? She had a very good education.'

'It's difficult', I said, 'to get into publishing. What is she doing now?'

'Secretary,' he said. 'In a chartered accountants' office, Gray's Inn. But I'd like to get her into publishing. She'd meet more cultured people, nicer people.'

'Cultured people are not necessarily nicer people,' I told him. 'Frequently, the reverse.'

'Oh,' he said, 'but surely in publishing you get to meet authors, artists, people of that kind? Interesting people, I mean.'

'Yes, that's true. But it's mostly dealing with books, not people.'

'I want Isobel to meet a better sort of people. Like yourself, Mrs Hawkins. I value your friendship with Isobel very much.'

Now, I had only a rooming-house acquaintance with young Isobel; and I could see that at least a part of dinner at the Savoy was in aid of my getting Isobel a job in publishing.

'I've lost my job in publishing,' I said. 'So I can't help.'

'Oh, you no longer work for that firm you were working for last week?'

'No longer. Anyway, I don't recommend publishing for your daughter. The secretaries are underpaid; everyone's underpaid.'

'Well, it's a sort of privilege job, isn't it?' he said.

Whatever it was we were eating I wasn't enjoying it. The candlelight and the wine and my black lace dress, Mr Lederer's white cuffs with gold cuff-links and his tanned, lined face seemed to accuse me of being there under false pretences. I began to remind myself that I was Mrs Hawkins and I didn't need a dinner at the Savoy, while Hugh Lederer proceeded with his protest to the effect that in a privileged job like publishing one didn't care about the pay.

'In Isobel's case the salary is a secondary consideration,' he said. 'It's a question of the elements. I'd like her to meet certain literary elements, more above the commercial, you realize, Mrs Hawkins. If you should hear of an opening –'

'I'll let you know if I hear of anything for Isobel but I'm looking for a job myself.'

The people at the other tables, in twos, fours, sixes, were having a good time. So I supposed. The people at the other tables always look happy by soft lights in those restaurants where the talk and tinkle are not too loud. I thought I, too, ought to feel tranquil with that looked-after sensation that good restaurants bring about. But I was uneasy, and perceived that Mr Lederer was aware of it. And at the same time, I must say, I felt sorry for him, with Isobel so much on his mind that he had to dine out so ambiguously for her.

'How did you come to lose your job so suddenly, Mrs Hawkins?'

I told him the story, across the elegant table.

'And what was that French name that you called the man? I didn't catch –'

'*Pisseur de copie.*'

'Which means?'

He knew what it meant but was hoping he was wrong.

I told him. And I said, 'In the literary world there are many *pisseurs de copie.*'

He was smiling feebly, overcome with great embarrassment. Which gave me a certain satisfaction.

'But Hector Bartlett is the top *pisseur* of our literary scene,' I said; and I only mentioned the name, Hector Bartlett, to give authenticity to my tale. I didn't expect him to know the name, but he did.

'Hector Bartlett. But Isobel knows him. She met him at a party or in a pub with some friends, and he's trying to get her a job in publishing, too. I haven't met him personally, but he has a certain influence. Only I thought that you, Mrs Hawkins, might be more in the know. Poor fellow, does he have a real problem of the bladder, then?'

'No, I was speaking metaphorically.'

Dance music was playing somewhere. I ate those small oblongs of toasted bread with oysters, anchovies and other involvements, called angels on horseback, which were then more commonly served at the end of a meal than they are now. Mr Lederer had a brandy.

'Isobel', he explained, 'likes artists and so on. She goes to those pubs and places where they all meet together and talk about culture. But I mustn't bore you.'

'Isobel should go to concerts, art galleries and poetry readings,' I said.

He got a taxi and insisted on taking me to the door.

'Good-night, Mrs Hawkins. It was nice to have your company.'

'Thank you very much, Mr Lederer.' Whether Isobel's daddy was married, divorced, widowed or simply a bachelor, I was never to know.

Indoors, there was a sound of revelry from Milly's kitchen. On investigation I found it did not arise from revelry but from consternation. Wanda's anonymous menacer had struck again, this time by telephone, only half an hour before, at quarter-past eleven. Wanda had roused the house and here she was, weeping and drinking tea, with Milly; with Basil and Eva Carlin, those quiet ones from the front bed-sitting-room; Kate Parker, the district nurse; with young Isobel, sleepy and yawning, her hand delicately patting her open mouth; with the medical student William Todd, fishing cotton wool out of an aspirin bottle; with, in fact, all of us. The Carlins wore Liberty dressing-gowns, looking better dressed than they did in the daytime, and in fact somewhat romantic. It occurred to me they were in love. Kate Parker had put on a white overall over her pyjamas. William Todd was wearing striped cotton pyjamas; his pocket didn't run to dressing-gowns. Wanda had on a purple taffeta kimono and Milly a blue silk one. And Isobel wore something of transparent pink nylon. I, in my black lace dress with my fur over my arm, caused a temporary silence, possibly astonishment. Then Wanda began, all over again, to tell her tearful story interspersed with the comments of the little crowd. Everyone had gone to bed. The telephone had rung. William had bolted down to answer. It was a man, urgently demanding Mrs Podolak. William had fetched her and started to climb the stairs to his room again. The house was then awakened by a long scream from Wanda.

All that was so far apparent from this event was that the tormentor was not one of the tenants and that he was a man.

Did she recognize the voice? – No, said Wanda.

A foreigner? – No.

'Well,' I said. 'We should inform the police.'

Wanda gave a long loud cry of No. 'Perhaps I know him. I can't place him,' she said.

Milly got out more cups and handed tea all round.

Before we sent Wanda to bed I gave her a notebook and

told her to write down as soon as possible everything she could remember about the voice, and what it said. 'I don't want to write down things,' said Wanda. I think already she had an inkling of who the voice belonged to. Perhaps, already, she had started putting two and two together.

Basil Carlin said confidingly to William Todd, 'Next thing he'll no doubt show up in person, and if I lay hands on him I'll black his eye.'

'I'd break his teeth,' said William.

Neither of them achieved these ambitions. Much of our time was to be taken up, and many wits were to be tried, in the effort to identify Wanda's tormentor. The idea hovered in the background of our lives for the next few months. But we were all too busy with the foreground of our lives to notice what was happening to Wanda.

But that night, while everyone was talking and exclaiming and putting forward theories, I went out in the garden by the kitchen door to admire the large bright moon which floodlit Milly's flower-beds, her beloved tall hollyhocks against the wall, and her pansy borders. The other houses in Church End Villas were all asleep. I was aware of a great lightness having fallen upon our house. I knew that it wasn't until this night's phone call had proved that nobody among us was responsible for Wanda's suffering that we realized the heaviness of the past six weeks. It is terrible to live with suspicions. Milly and I had privately scrutinized everyone, and now it came to me that each and everyone in the house, Milly excepted, had inevitably suspected, not only each other, but had also wondered about me.

Hector Bartlett was already far from my thoughts; there was

no possible way I could have thought of him in connection with Wanda, not having yet come across that glint of a thin trail, like something a snail leaves in its slow path, which led from him to Wanda. But even if I had known, it would have been irrelevant to my feelings of relief: the persecutor was not one of us, not one of us.

Now, to cheer things up still further, someone had turned on the wireless to Radio Luxembourg with its late-night dance music. I could hear Milly begging everyone to keep it low. I could hear the tinkle of tea-cups and the voices loosening up in prattle in the kitchen; the household was garrulous with tacit deliverance. Even Wanda, now upstairs, had stopped wailing; she came down again only to proclaim, in a very insistent voice that reached me in the garden, her oft-repeated assertion that her persecutor was an agent of the Red Dean (as was known the widely deplored, the learned and the communist, then Dean of Canterbury).

Suddenly William Todd came out to the garden. 'What a moon!' he said. He took my hand and put his other arm round my large waist as far as it could reach, and danced me all over the lawn to the sound of the music, he in his cotton pyjamas and I, Mrs Hawkins, in my black lace party dress.

6

While waiting for another job I considered myself on holiday; I painted my rooms at Church End Villas and put up new curtains. I found a job for Cathy as book-keeper and invoice-clerk, not with a publisher as she wanted, but with a small printer at Notting Hill, a kindly man who knew of our troubles at Ullswater Press, although it was actually through Milly that she got the job. And it was through Kate, the district nurse, that I got mine.

When you are looking for a job the best thing to do is to tell everyone, high and humble, and keep reminding them please to look out for you. This advice is not guaranteed to find you a job, but it is remarkable how suitable jobs can be found through the most unlikely people. For instance, if you are looking for a job as a management consultant or a television announcer, and can do the job, you will naturally apply · for the jobs available, advertised in the normal papers, known to the appropriate agencies and to friends in the field of business. But you should also tell the postman, the mechanic in the garage, the waiter in the restaurant, the hotel porter, the grocer, the butcher, the daily domestic help; you should tell everyone, including people you meet on the train.

It is surprising how many people subterraneously believe in destiny. The word goes round, and in a relaxed moment a businessman will listen with interest to the barman or the doorman. Hearing of the very person he is looking for, he might well think that luck has come his way, and arrange to see the applicant next day. There is involved that fine feeling and boast: 'I just happened to be looking for an accountant, and do you know I got a first-class fellow through the barman at the Goat.' People love coincidence, destiny, a lucky chance. It is worth telling everyone if you want a job. In any case, while you are looking for a job you are always walking in the dark.

So it came about that Milly's friend and neighbour Mrs Twinny, with whom she went to Bingo every Thursday afternoon, heard from Milly that I was called to the phone a great deal by a certain Cathy, a book-keeper in my former office, and that Cathy gave me little peace, she was looking for another job in publishing. Mrs Twinny remarked that Mr Twinny was putting in shelves for a publisher. In fact, she meant a printer, it came to the same thing. Milly reported this conversation to me, with dramatic eagerness a few days later; it came with the news that Mr Twinny had procured an interview for Cathy. 'Funnily enough he's looking for a book-keeper,' said Milly, 'and he's looking for someone he can trust, with a recommendation. They have to handle cash.' So it was that I took Cathy on the bus to Notting Hill. Cathy had at first put up a resistance to applying for the job on the

64

grounds that a printer in London W.8 was not the same as a publisher in W.1. I had met her at five-thirty near South Kensington station in one of the new espresso-bars that were then opening up all over London. She was still with Ullswater Press but knew it was doomed; she knew it only too well from the books she had to try to keep. She looked at me over the cappuccino raised to her lips, with her puckered face and balding dyed hair; she looked at me through her thick lenses and said, 'I should put my head in the gas oven.'

I didn't think for a minute that she would get the job. But I went along with her to the interview and she got it. And the only thing that could explain why she was taken on the spot, apart from her honesty which I had vouched for in a simple letter of recommendation (in place of one from Martin York which I didn't feel would get Cathy very far, so near was he to the hour of his reckoning for fraud), was a certain superstition on the part of Mr Wells, the printer. I waited for Cathy in the noisy outer workshop, sitting on a chair which had been dusted specially for me. Mr Wells came out with Cathy, both smiling. 'A most extraordinary coincidence,' he said. 'This man was putting up shelves, and we were having a chat at the coffee break, and he happened to remark . . .' I assume the hiring of Cathy became his favourite anecdote. She kept the job for twelve years, retiring on the death of her employer.

I happened to get a job for Patrick very easily, having been actually asked by a bookseller in the Charing Cross Road, when I was in his shop one day rummaging around the second-hand shelves, if I knew of a young man capable of minding the shop, selling books and also packaging and posting the mail orders. But this brought on my head a series of reactions from his wife, Mabel, who rang me every day and sometimes twice on the same day with alternating expressions of gratitude and reproach. First I was a wonderful woman to have done this great good deed for Patrick, especially as he now got more pay; and secondly I was a fat old whore who was never done trying to wheedle him into my bed with my wiles and favours. For Patrick's sake I tried to humour her as long as I could. I hardly listened to her on the phone, so that my answers didn't always correspond to what she was saying: 'It was a pleasure, Mabel. No trouble on my part. I hope everything will go well with you, now,' I said, once, when she was actually accusing me of 'doing it upside down' with her husband.

Milly, when she answered the phone to Mabel, threatened to report her to the police, refused to call me to the phone. I went to see Patrick in the book shop: 'Patrick, you have to take Mabel to a doctor.' 'She won't go,' he said, and was close to tears.

On some of those days before I got my next job I went for long walks, whatever the weather, discovering scenes and aspects of London which office-workers never see. I recall a day when there must have been fine weather, for in a street at Regent's Park a film was being made for which artificial rain was made to fall in great quantities.

'What between Mabel and her phone calls and those anonymous letters and calls for Wanda, the house is a nightmare,' Milly said. 'Pack a bag, Mrs Hawkins. I'm taking you home for a fortnight.'

'Home' to Milly was Cork. I willingly accepted and enjoyed a summer holiday in the fine rain and sunshine of Ireland, remote from mad and untrustworthy London among people who acknowledged respectfully the cultural life but were not remotely mixed up with it. Milly's eldest daughter lived with her husband in a new house on the outskirts of Cork from which every day we set out for some new stretch of Southern Irish greenery. At night I would lie awake as long as possible with the sound in my mind's ear of soft voices and amusing stories and in my mind's eye an ambience of leafiness. Sometimes I thought of London and wondered where fate would take me in the future, and sometimes in those precious, silent, waking hours I thought of Wanda. And I thought then more clearly than before. I felt she was now holding something back, that she was not still unaware as she said she was as to the possible identity of her enemy. Since that night of the anonymous phone call she claimed there had arrived another letter, but she didn't show it around. According to Wanda, the writer had changed the motive of his threats. It was no longer the income tax, it was something else. About the phone call she was imprecise. This led me to reflect that in any case the man now knew that her little tax affair had been put right. But Wanda was still upset, very distressed. She had wept when I went to say good-bye before I left for Ireland, and I thought she was going to tell me something; but she hesitated and decided not. I didn't press. Indeed, in a sense I didn't want to know, for I felt the weight of so many of other people's difficulties. I was still young, in my twenties, and everyone treated me like a matronly goddess of wisdom. I fell asleep one night, thinking of my own future and its possibilities and with the strange, involuntary image of the moonlit garden at Church End Villas, that night of the anonymous phone call to

Wanda, after my dinner at the Savoy; and I thought of William Todd whirling me round and round.

When Milly and I got back home only one thing had changed and it didn't affect us very much: a reshuffle of personnel in the house next door. Marky's wife and baby had left and another girl, still 'my wife' to Marky, with two children and a young sister had taken their place; the first sister-in-law remained: an interesting mixture; Milly speculated much on the outcome.

Ian Tooley, director of the vast publishing firm of Mackintosh & Tooley, looked at his pocket diary and said, 'I suggest you start next Monday, the 11th, Mrs Hawkins. If that is convenient?' I said that would suit me very well. It was a week ahead. 'You will find us at the peak of our activity,' he said, his eye still on the page of his diary. 'October 12th will be the next day, Tuesday, a full moon: there will be a movement of authors.'

'Do you find the moon affects the authors, Mr Tooley?' I said.

'Oh, a great deal, believe me,' he said deeply. 'There is always a considerable movement from those quarters at the full moon.'

This saying, combined with the décor of the office, made me extraordinarily happy: I knew already that the new job was going to be something of an adventure.

I hadn't expected to get the job. In fact I suspected that a number of highly experienced men and women editors must have applied for it, people with recommendations, qualifications, honours degrees, specializations, and after I had been at the job for some time I found out that this was true. Many well-known reviewers and literary editors and BBC personnel had applied for this job at Mackintosh & Tooley, and had been interviewed for it. It was later that I realized why I was employed in preference to these impressive applications.

I got the job at Mackintosh & Tooley in October through Kate, who had been nursing an elderly relation-by-marriage of Sir Alec Tooley throughout September. Martin York had already been arrested for fraud and was now remanded on bail and in a nursing home tended by psychiatrists.

The scandal in the publishing world was rife, and the bankruptcy of the Ullswater Press and his other ventures, imminent and inevitable. A considerable list of people stood to lose weighty sums of money in the crash.

To entertain her patient, whom Kate greatly liked, she read bits of *The Times* to her every day, I imagine with those appropriate observations of a moral order, so typical of Kate. And, according to Kate, the news of Martin York's arrest with the list of his alleged (as the papers put it at this stage) frauds and forgeries, so much fascinated Kate's patient that Kate was led to say she knew someone who had, up to only recently, been an editor at the Ullswater Press, and was alas out of work.

This news was passed on rapidly to Sir Alec Tooley. I believe his sick relation must have been a fairly poor relation, otherwise she would have had a private nurse, not Kate. I suspect that this near-acquaintance with an actual inside observer of the goings-on at Martin York's establishment was a kind of poor relation's offering to the rich Sir Alec, and that he in turn was induced by curiosity to arrange an interview for me. This is my construction of how I got the interview, for certainly there was a vacancy for an editor just then, and the candidates were many and the qualifications required were far higher than any I could claim. Some series of reasons and half-reasons like this procured me the interview. Why I actually got the job was, I am sure, due to something else. Kate had warned me fairly: 'These are different people than you meet every day, Mrs Hawkins. They can command university degrees and titled young lads as their office boys.'

But allowing for the rhetoric of Kate's sincere beliefs, it was still a mystery to me that I got the job. I came to realize the answer later.

I had been interviewed by two directors in turn. Ian Tooley, of Mackintosh & Tooley, son of Sir Alec Tooley (there was no surviving Mackintosh), an esoteric crank, was the second. First, I had been ushered in to the vast carpeted office of Sir Alec. I was fairly keyed up, so I didn't notice many details at first. An elderly man. A voice that I placed at the back of my mind as surprising, a whimper. I was too occupied with the interview and whether I could possibly hope to get a job in this important firm of publishers to take in much as Sir Alec talked.

'Mrs Hawkins, I believe you in fact worked for the Ullswater Press? That must have been an interesting experience,' he prompted me.

I said that it was.

'And what was your feeling about Mr York's conduct?'

I said I thought Martin York was off his head if it were proved he forged documents without taking the slightest precaution to conceal his own handwriting. 'But', I said, 'my work at Ullswater Press was with actual books.'

'Ah yes, in fact, books,' said the venerable publisher. 'Yes, many of our staff here are in fact fairly interested in books. One of our senior colleagues in fact was saying at a meeting only the other day that he thought he might perhaps have a shot at getting back to his first love – *books*. Now, tell me, in fact, Mrs Hawkins . . .'

I had begun to wonder if I had wandered into the wrong premises. Was it tomato soup, ladies' dresses, washing machines that they trafficked in here? But Sir Alec pressed on '. . . was there not in fact – I am sure you must know – some difficulty or *fracas* at the shareholders' meetings?'

I told him I was never at the shareholders' meetings, but according to the newspapers there was a lot of money involved.

'Indeed there is, Mrs Hawkins. Distilleries, building schemes. I quite understand you, in fact, wanting to keep out of it, although let me assure you that anything you say between these four walls will go no further. Given that York is a loony and I'm not, in fact, excluding it, tell me about Ted Ullswater. I suppose he's taken the affair rather hard?'

I was now noticing rather more. On his desk was a silver frame with the photograph of a woman of the 'twenties in Court dress holding an ostrich-feather fan.

Sir Alec was thin and grey and his voice matched his looks. It sounded like a wisp of smoke wafting from some burning of leaves hidden by a clump of lavender. The effort that appeared to go into his voice seemed not to correspond with any commensurable weariness or boredom; indeed, he was eager to pump me, and, genuinely looking for a job as I was, I felt highly impatient both with the affectation built in to his manner and with the fact that I had come primed for a serious interview and was being frivolously quizzed. Moreover, I had come in a taxi. I always took a taxi to an interview.

I said I understood there was an editorial job available.

'Yes,' he breathed, 'there is in fact an editorial job available, I believe.' He pressed a button on his desk and spoke through an intercom. 'Ian, would you come in please? I have a lady editor who might in fact very well suit us. Yes, now, please.'

He rose and so did I. He walked me to the door just as it opened and Ian Tooley came in. Sir Alec offered me a limp hand and when I took it he seemed to throw my hand away into thin air. 'Ian, this is Mrs Hawkins.' Then he said to me, or rather sighed out the words: 'I hope you don't believe that Shakespeare wrote the plays. The evidence in fact does not stand independent scrutiny. He must be laughing up his sleeve in the next world, if in fact there is one, when he looks down and sees what is in fact going on at Stratford-on-Avon.'

I followed Ian Tooley along a carpeted corridor, its walls lined with reproductions of the Boz illustrations of Dickens, into his own less vast but impressively oak-panelled office.

Ian Tooley was more robust than his father whom he resembled except that he appeared to have a squint, which presently I found was not so; it was an effect caused by his nose going off at a slight angle. Unlike his father he was casually dressed in a sports jacket and brown corduroy trousers, unusual for office-wear in those days. More unusual still, he wore a vivid green tie. I thought, after all he might be interesting.

He began by looking at me very closely, very carefully, not at all as a man looks at a woman but as if he were considering me as a specimen for some purpose quite beyond my understanding. I felt dreadfully physical.

'You worked for the self-styled financial genius, Martin York?' he said.

'I was an editor in the publishing firm. They published some good books,' I said.

'Well then, you understand about proof-reading, dealing with authors, et cetera, et cetera.'

'All that,' I said, without any clear idea what the et ceteras meant.

Now I was anxious to get away; convinced they had only got me to come along out of curiosity, and that they were in any case looking for an honours graduate or someone of that nature.

A tall thin girl came in with a tray of tea, set out with a silver tea-pot and delicate china. 'Thank you, Abigail. May I introduce Mrs Hawkins, who is coming to join us – Abigail de Mordell Staines-Knight.'

That was how I knew I had got the job. Miss de Mordell Staines-Knight swept me a small smile over her shoulder, for she had already started to leave the room.

'Abigail', said Ian Tooley when she had gone, 'is a Virgo.'

My alarm at this saying was allayed by his going on to expound some part of his astral studies, promising me that he would have my full horoscope cast as soon as I could provide him with the exact hour and minute of my birth and that of my mother and father. Their birthdays and mine, he assured me, were not enough. One needed the hours, the minutes. And he ended the interview with the words I have already recorded: 'I suggest you start next Monday . . . October 12 will be the next day, Tuesday, a full moon . . . a movement of authors.'

I believe it was only part-consciously that Ian Tooley, who was in charge of taking on the senior personnel, invariably chose someone, in some respect, not quite normal.

Because the office was peopled, although inefficiently, by a staff of secretaries, book-keepers, filing clerks, typists, according to their various departments, all of average tastes and appearance, it was some time before I noticed that those who were in charge, who administrated or had to deal with agents or authors especially, were in some way handicapped and vulnerable, either physically or in some other of their circumstances. My awareness was gradual, because of the spontaneous sympathy these colleagues of mine evoked. It was when I had begun to piece together the possible motive for their having been appointed to their jobs in the first place, unconscious though it might be, that I wondered what was 'wrong' with myself.

This process of increasing realization on my part took some months. Right away I could be in no doubt that the office was run by agreeable people. Only, one way and another one was obliged to feel sorry for them or embarrassed in their innocent company. It was abundantly difficult to find fault, disagree or show any impatience with these people. I didn't try. But those who did try, outsiders for the most part – printers, authors, binders, agents – seemed to place themselves in the light of brutes, and probably felt themselves to be so.

Among the senior staff was a charming doctor of fifty who had been struck off the rolls, an accountant with a thin, white face who had a dreadful stammer and who said the most agree-able things when he did at last, word by word, form a sentence; my fellow-editor was a sweet-natured, though vague, young woman, a vicar's daughter, her face frightfully marred all one side by a port-wine birth-mark. The head of the pro-duction department, totally incompetent but very witty, had a duodenal ulcer which he bore bravely, and limped from a war-wound. Ian Tooley's fellow-director and next-in-command was equally nice. We saw little of her. She worked largely behind the scenes but when she made an appearance to deal with a specially difficult problem or to arrange an important contract for a best-seller with a high-powered agent, she was treated with hushed deference, tough business-woman though she was; she was the daughter of a notorious mass-murderer of the early 'thirties; her father had been hanged; nobody could be tough with her.

There was also, attached to the firm and often in evidence, a very small, raddled and parchment-faced photographer who called himself Vladimir, a White Russian, who was said to beat his mother. He had a small retainer fee from Mackintosh & Tooley, and his job was to photograph authors in the most 'interesting' which is to say unbecoming and grotesque aspects. Those foolish enough to sit for him were reproduced on the book-jackets. The rejected photographs Vladimir sold to a clandestine shop in Soho for a modest fee, so supple-menting the pittance he derived from Mackintosh & Tooley and a few other publishers who desired to take their authors – always, to them, overweening – down a peg. Vladimir had an unfortunate destiny; he died of leukemia three years later, in 1957, at which point he turned out to be not Vladimir of

White Russian princely origin, but Cyril Biggs from Wandsworth. But in 1954 he flourished and was an obliging ally to Mackintosh & Tooley. I think if there had existed a known descendant of Jack the Ripper they would have taken him on. It was their way of doing business as surely as cripple-dom, in the Far East, is still a profession and a way of life.

Ian Tooley himself was his own alibi. Vegetarian, graphol-ogist and astrologist, he would put all trouble and vexation down to the stars rising in a certain sign or a phase of the moon. All ailments were caused by meat-eating, and these he held could be cured by a combination of vegetable diet and radionics. This latter treatment was, and still is, known as the Box. Ian Tooley possessed a Box and had trained his secretary, the tall, charming Abigail de Mordell Staines-Knight, to oper-ate it. Ian Tooley proclaimed her to be highly talented at Box-operating, or radionics as he called it; and this, apart from her bringing in to him (but not making) a tray of morning coffee and one of afternoon tea, was her entire job. As it hap-pened, Abigail didn't believe in radionics. She thought the Box was a complete fake. She only did this job because it was to her a merry, effortless occupation, a joke for which she got paid.

The Box was in fact a small black box about the size of a dressing case. The Tooley model, one of the first of its kind, opened up to reveal a row of different coloured lights and a few knobs. There was a place for inserting a piece of hair or a blood-smear, and this was supposed to cure the ailments of those from whom the blood or the hair had been taken. I am describing my first sight of the electronic Box, as Abigail showed it and explained it to me, with a sort of casual solemnity. So far as I could see it was as devoid of any functional possibility as one of those children's toy telephones which they go through the motions of dialling a number and talking, but never get anywhere. That was at first sight, and I will say here that at last sight (only the other day) and after much study of radionics literature, the more elaborate and complicated instrument seemed to me equally unserviceable. At the time Abigail showed me her Box I was somewhat relieved to find it futile, because, as I pointed out, if the Box could do good it could also do evil. 'It stands to reason,' I said.

'Oh,' said Abigail de Mordell Staines-Knight, 'how right you are. But don't let Ian hear you say so. To him, it's impossible to do anything wrong with the Box. And in fact, it does nobody any harm, let's face it.'

She was a really nice girl in spite of her name. I, too, didn't think you could do wrong with the Box, nor right with it, nor anything. I was more curious to know what, in reality, Ian Tooley fancied she was doing with it. Who, at the behest of Ian Tooley, was she aiming to affect or cure?

'It's rather confidential,' she said, shyly.

Those strange memories I have retained of Mackintosh & Tooley are, however, overspread with a sort of tenderness. I know I shouldn't have liked being there as much as I did, for the happiness of the firm was based first on the happiness of its members and only second on principles. Principles were the last thing anybody bothered about, although it was a very different establishment from that of the Ullswater Press, in that, for one thing, Mackintosh & Tooley flourished in their business affairs and were prosperous. But the mere fact of being able to balance your books and do good trade doesn't mean that you are a person of moral principle. And in many ways poor Martin York was more principled than the Tooleys.

Often, now, in my beloved insomnia I recall the fine old offices of Mackintosh & Tooley, in a street off Covent Garden, those high-ceilinged offices which, eighteen years later when Mackintosh & Tooley merged and moved in with another publisher, were gutted and made modern, and even the exterior was fresh-painted and hardly recognizable to me, passing it in the street.

I see again, in my wide-eyed midnights, my own small office which looked out into the well of a back courtyard, and was ill-lit; but it felt good to have an office to myself, a step up in the world. Here I dealt with new and aspiring writers, in other words the authors; for generally the writers published by Mackintosh & Tooley were placed into two categories: Authors and Names. The latter were the few established living authors on the firm's list, and these Names dealt with Ann Clough whose father, though completely crazy, had nonetheless been hanged.

My editorial colleague's name was Connie, she with the port-wine birth-mark on her face and a timid vague air; try as I do, I can't recall her surname. Indeed, her very abstractedness and insubstantial personality seemed to say 'forget me'; she seemed to live in parenthesis; but I haven't forgotten her, only her surname. And even the birth-mark on her face became unnoticeable as I got used to her, as blemishes do.

Connie occupied the office next door to mine. She received the manuscripts of new authors, glanced at them and, if they were fairly literate, sent them out to be reported on by readers who were mainly retired and indigent unmarried people who lived in the country, had a certain amount of education, were glad of the occupation and the extra money, and who were supposed to represent the average reader. Connie enjoyed a prolific correspondence with these readers. Their lengthy reports were generally gloomy, beginning with phrases like 'I'm afraid that *The Café on the Corner* is hardly a masterpiece . . .' or 'This novel is not to be recommended. The sordid element in some of the scenes cannot be redeemed by the seriousness of the subject-matter.' A synopsis of the story would follow at the undisciplined length of four or five pages. The end of the report would invariably be a paragraph of one sentence, put in for effect, such as: 'No, and again, no, to your novel, Mr Travers,' or 'This author should definitely be rebuffed.' These scornful missives were, however, enlivened for Connie by an accompanying letter informing her of the weather in Shropshire, the progress of the roses and geraniums, the nephews, the nieces and occasionally an ailing mother. Connie would reply to these pen-friends cheerily and at length, as soon as she had finished sending to the packing department the condemned manuscripts, with a rejection slip, there to be dispatched to their owners. God knows if any masterpieces were actually lost to the public through this means of selection. I wonder how many of the aspiring writers of those days still have in a drawer the leaf-eared typescripts that they sent to sea in a sieve.

Connie's other job was proof-editing, which she did very badly. Transferring the author's corrections to a clean sheet of proofs was something Connie was unable to do without missing an average of three corrections a page, or transcribing newly inserted material all wrong. In those days the authors had long galley-proofs followed by page-proofs. It was only when the book finally appeared that Connie's mistakes were discovered, but she was incorporeal about them. She put angry authors' letters about the mutilation of their books under the cushion of her chair to deal with later; she timidly suggested to their irate voices on the phone that they should write a letter putting down their grievances which would be attended to in the next edition. But if they insisted on calling in to see her face-to-face, the authors were so overcome by the first sight of Connie's poor port-wine mark that their rage immediately subsided. You couldn't be nasty to Connie, and a friendly arrangement was always reached by Connie's gossamer-voiced assurance that the matter would be put right in the next printing. Since the next printing hardly ever happened that was safe enough.

Sometimes an author's agent would go over Connie's head and complain about Connie, as when she overlooked a printer's error on the first page of a book, which had been corrected accurately by the author, and by which a 'blond' man became a 'blind' man, so that nobody could make head or tail of the subsequent story. Situations like these were smoothed over by an expensive lunch given to the agent by breezy Colin Shoe, he who had been scored off the medical register, and whatever the outcome of these peace-revels, none of it reached the ears or the desk of Connie. 'We can't have our staff upset,' many a time was one of the statements of charming Colin Shoe.

I used to spend my coffee-break and my tea-time with Connie, sometimes in her office, sometimes in mine. My job was to collect from her those few new manuscripts that had a faint possibility of being shaped into a book for publication, or whose authors should perhaps be nurtured. It was a very tentative affair, as Colin Shoe put it. I had to talk to authors. Colin didn't, he said, envy me my job, amiably adding one of his more regular maxims, 'The best author is a dead author.' And it is true we would have had an easier time if we only had the books to deal with and no live authors; Mackintosh & Tooley had a small back-list of dead writers who caused very little trouble (except occasionally through their heirs and executors, who got taken out to lunches if they became too difficult).

I was quite aware of this feeling, at the same time that I wanted human contact in my work.

'Books don't wriggle. Authors do,' was one of Colin Shoe's remarks. 'They take everything personally,' Colin Shoe would say. 'There isn't an author who doesn't take their books personally.' I felt this was obviously a virtue on the author's part; but, at the same time, these airily expressed prejudices gave us of the firm a coterie sensation which, amoral as it was, I shouldn't have liked but rather did.

But I was glad of my authors, admitted that most of them were more or less *pisseurs de copie*. 'In a way,' said Colin, 'you're lucky to have authors, not Names, to deal with.' He was full of euphoria at that moment, for he was about to lunch with famous Emma Loy who had hinted she might want to bring her next novel to Mackintosh & Tooley. Colin Shoe made a great occasion of his heavy responsibility in connection with this new Name. I earnestly hoped that Colin's efforts would fail and Emma Loy take her book elsewhere.

I invited the new and aspiring authors to visit me. A few of them I had already been in correspondence with when I was at the Ullswater Press. I rigged up an electric hot-plate and a kettle in a corner of my office and so was able to offer tea and biscuits in the afternoon, coffee and biscuits in the morning, without applying to the typists who usually prepared the office teas and coffees. I suppose I must have been a formidable, somewhat maternal figure while I dished out tea, biscuits and advice. I can see now those men and women, mainly young, who came one by one, twice, three times a week to sit in the armchair I had placed for them and listen to what I had to say about their manuscripts. Very, very few were destined to make a literary career, but a great many of them were far better informed than I was, which made it difficult for me to deal with clever authors of uncertain talent. I have always been free with advice; but it is one thing to hand out advice and another to persuade people to accept it. At Mackintosh & Tooley, at this stage, my large presence assisted me sometimes but not always.

I remember random scenes and I also remember my subsequent memories; so that I recall that I was lying awake in the dark, about ten years ago, when to my mind came the image of a meeting I had had in my office at Mackintosh & Tooley with a young man, one of the most beautiful I have ever seen, the author of a large novel about nothing in particular. It proved only that he passionately wanted to write, and I told him we couldn't take the book but he should try another, more concise, not so long and rambling, and about something in particular. I recall very little else of that interview but that he embarked on a lengthy discourse, citing famous long novels about nothing in particular. Had I read *Finnegans Wake*?

I had to admit I hadn't, not from cover to cover. I didn't know at the time that very few people had.

He spoke for an hour. He accepted my coffee and biscuits and went on talking. I wish I could remember more of what he said; it was extremely above my head. Had I read *Buddenbrooks* by Thomas Mann?

I hadn't but I had heard of it. I evaded the question by taking a chance: 'But that is about something in particular.'

He said it contained nothing but details, and went on. Had I read Proust?

Yes, I had read Proust.

'And you say it's about something in particular?'

It was twelve noon. *The angel of the Lord brought the tidings* . . . 'Well, it's about everything in particular, isn't it?'

The word was made flesh . . .

'Well, my novel is about everything in particular.'

Hail Mary, full of grace . . .

'So it is,' I said. 'But it isn't Proust.'

'So you're looking for another Proust?' he said. 'One isn't enough?'

I forget how I got him out of the office; I only remember his going. I recall that the date was 1st November and that an evening paper showed the portrait of Winston Churchill by Graham Sutherland which was presented to him by the Houses of Parliament, and which, after his death years later, his wife awesomely destroyed; and I wonder in the night what her real reason was. I wonder, too, what has happened to the beautiful young man and his large book, so large that he had to hold it in two parts, one under each arm, as he left the office.

Now, it fell to me to give advice to many authors which in at least two cases bore fruit. So I will repeat it here, free of charge. It proved helpful to the type of writer who has some imagination and wants to write a novel but doesn't know how to start.

'You are writing a letter to a friend,' was the sort of thing I used to say. 'And this is a dear and close friend, real – or better – invented in your mind like a fixation. Write privately, not publicly; without fear or timidity, right to the end of the letter, as if it was never going to be published, so that your true friend will read it over and over, and then want more enchanting letters from you. Now, you are not writing about the relationship between your friend and yourself; you take that for granted. You are only confiding an experience that you think only he will enjoy reading. What you have to say will come out more spontaneously and honestly than if you are thinking of numerous readers. Before starting the letter rehearse in your mind what you are going to tell; something interesting, your story. But don't rehearse too much, the story will develop as you go along, especially if you write to a special friend, man or woman, to make them smile or laugh or cry, or anything you like so long as you know it will interest. Remember not to think of the reading public, it will put you off.'

In the two cases where this method succeeded with first novels they did very well. It was also successful in other cases with short stories.

On 1st December Martin York was sentenced to his seven years' imprisonment. Later, for Christmas, I wrote to him at

Wormwood Scrubs but like so many others who had written, I got no reply. He had gone into the shadows. The day after the sentence the papers were full of articles by some of his former acquaintances testifying to his chaotic world, his boyish charm, his reckless drinking and spending, his wild schemes and ambitions to become a world tycoon. Among the writers of the articles were some who I knew had been heavily in Martin's debt. There was the first of many pieces by Hector Bartlett. He insinuated without actually stating, that he himself had been a victim of Martin York's fraudulence, which I knew to be totally untrue.

In those sad days of early December I began to compare in my mind the two publishing houses that fate had led me to. Before I fell asleep at Church End Villas, South Kensington, I would lie, looking at the darkness for at least an hour, recalling the noise, and the frantic, fugitive atmosphere of Ullswater Press. Cathy the book-keeper, Ivy the telephonist and typist, the packer and his visiting wife Mabel, wild-eyed and accusing. The wear and tumble of a sinking firm, and Martin York sitting in his chair, needing company. There had been a great deal wrong with the business, but was there anything more wrong with the people themselves than there was with the elite company at the far grander and money-stable Mackintosh & Tooley? It seemed to me more than ever that the staff at Mackintosh & Tooley had been deliberately chosen for some slightly grotesque quality; and although these were all much better qualified, educated, and led more facilitated and privileged lives than those poorly paid hands at the late Ullswater Press, there was really something saner and healthier about the Ullswater staff. They had their oddities but they had been chosen in spite of, not because of them.

Reflecting thus, one night I was suddenly moved to switch on the light, get out of bed and look at myself in the long glass on the inside of my clothes cupboard. I stood there, massive in my loose, warm nightdress. What was wrong with me? Why had I been chosen by Mackintosh & Tooley? It was then the reason dawned on me: I was immensely too fat. I was overweight, I thought, to the point that anyone employing me must be kinky. It was plain to me that no-one who had a complaint to utter or anything against the firm, especially an aggrieved author, could express themselves strongly to me. It would have been unkind. It would have been like attacking their mother. Above all, it would have looked bad. I was one of the Mackintosh & Tooley alibis.

From that night I decided to eat and drink half. Only half of everything I normally ate, in any circumstances. And I decided to tell nobody at all about my plan. Just to say, if pressed, that I'd had enough. And just to consume half, or perhaps even a quarter, until I reached a reasonable weight and size. And I started next morning eating less, drinking less.

The act fitted in with my sadness in those early days of December 1954. Not many days later, just as I was leaving the office, came a screaming phone call from Mabel with her usual accusations. Patrick evidently came into the room from where she was phoning, for he shouted above her voice into the phone. 'Take no notice, Mrs Hawkins. Please take no offence. Mabel's not well.'

I thought he meant not well in the head, which she obviously wasn't. I said, 'Mabel must see a psychiatrist.'

'I'm going into hospital tomorrow,' Mabel said, more quietly. 'And, Mrs Hawkins, you've been so good to Patrick. I only wish you wouldn't sleep with him in your spare time.'

She was operated on next day, poor young woman, but nothing could have saved her from the galloping malignant disease that she died of within a week. I visited her twice in the hospital. She recognized me, but was glazed and doped. I went to her cremation at Golders Green and seeing her coffin slide away, I regretted I had ever thought ill of Mabel, or treated her like the nuisance she had been. Oh Mabel, come back; come back, Mabel, and persecute me again. Patrick cried all the way through. He told me, 'I knew she had mental trouble. But she was always all right physically. This came on so quick, so quick, Mrs Hawkins.'

7

To my great joy my black lace evening dress needed to be taken in a good inch both sides when, in January of 1955, I tried it on with a view to wearing it at a smart dinner party, how smart, I did not quite know until I got there. In fact, until I got there I didn't realize it was my first smart London dinner party. Up to that time I had been out to dinner a great many times, at friends' private houses or in restaurants. But never, so far, on such a formal occasion.

The invitation card was on my desk one morning, 'Mr Ian and Lady Philippa Tooley request the pleasure of the company of Mrs Hawkins . . .' At the lower corner were the words 'Black tie', which I knew to mean I had to wear an evening dress; but that was all I knew. I explained to Milly, who handled the invitation with interest, that the black tie was what the men had to wear. I replied that Mrs Hawkins had pleasure in accepting Mr Ian and Lady Philippa Tooley's kind invitation . . . And there I was in Wanda's room, having my black lace dress pinned and tucked, and the neckline cut low, with a view to its being reduced to my latest size and remodelled, as Wanda put it, to bring it up to date.

Wanda's room was still the workshop of old. Piles of clothes to be altered, and among them another dress of mine. She often altered dresses for me, but this was the first time she had to take one in.

'I have such terrible rheumatism,' said Wanda, who was on her knees, with her pins, sticking them abundantly into my dress. 'I'm behind with my work.' I told her the lace dress was urgent.

It was difficult for her to move. She was having treatment, she said.

'What treatment are you getting?'

Wanda evaded the question; and perhaps, I felt, I was too inquisitive. All Wanda said was, 'It takes time . . . got to have faith.'

But I couldn't forbear to pass her a piece of advice. 'Rheumatism, Wanda,' I said, 'takes many forms. I hope you've got a good doctor. However, whatever it is you're taking for your rheumatism, believe me, it's a great help to eat a banana a day.' I myself had suffered attacks of rheumatic pain two years before and on the advice of an American negress whom I met in the bus, I had started on the cure of a banana every day, since when I had felt no further pains in my legs. All this I told to Wanda while she was snipping round my neckline. (I omitted to tell her that for the past six weeks I had eaten but half a banana a day.) But Wanda only frowned, creaking herself to her feet. I noticed her head shifted jerkily towards a point on the floor below the window. Wanda was still haunted; all her old confidence and tranquillity had left her. Now, as I turned round at her request for some further pinning-up, I saw, under the window on the floor, a black leather-covered case, very much resembling Ian Tooley's radionic Box. I thought it so unlikely that Wanda, a fervent cult-Catholic, would have any traffic with the Box that I felt this was some other container with fittings, some sewing or dressing-case.

Wanda said, 'How did you come to lose the inches, Mrs Hawkins?'

'Nature is adjusting itself,' I said. 'And not before time.'

I was still automatically studying the black case under the window; Wanda's hands trembled a little with her pins. This was unlike her.

On the chance that Wanda's box was truly the Box, I said, 'You work the Box?'

'What box?' said Wanda. She had turned scared. I thought she was going to give that cry of hers.

'I mean a box that is used in what people call radionics. They claim to cure people, and presumably do other things.'

'Other things?'

'One would suppose . . . But anyhow, I don't believe in it.'

'I don't know about Box. Maybe you get a bit thinner still, Mrs Hawkins?'

'Oh, yes,' I said. 'I hope to lose a lot more weight.' I felt quite hungry as I said it with the prospect of months ahead of eating half. But I didn't tell Wanda my secret, and she didn't tell me any more of hers.

I gave the Box a rather contemptuous glance when I left, dramatically hoping Wanda would notice it. It seemed to me that Wanda was now afraid of me and regretted her half-confidence.

'I need another fitting for your dress, Mrs Hawkins. I

promise it comes out lovely. Another fitting, tomorrow night. Keep well.'

What did she mean: keep well?

I was touchy at that time. Who should ring me up, just as I was getting ready to go to the Tooleys' dinner party, but Isobel's Daddy?

'Good evening, Mrs Hawkins, Hugh Lederer speaking.'

'Yes, Mr Lederer?'

'You sound as if you're in a hurry.'

'I am, rather. I'm going out to dinner.'

'Well, lucky man, whoever he is. I saw you in church last Sunday but you didn't see me.'

'No, I didn't see you.'

'You were in a hurry, then, too. And if I might say so you were looking very pretty.'

It was true that the loss of ten pounds' weight was beginning to give my bone-structure a chance. I was glad to hear this speech of Hugh Lederer, but I had a good idea what he was ringing me about: Isobel's problem.

'I really am in rather a hurry, now, Mr Lederer. I have to get dressed, and –'

'Mrs Hawkins, will you dine with me tomorrow?'

'I'm afraid I can't.'

'Friday, then?'

'Is it about Isobel?'

'Well,' he said, 'that's one of the things.'

'I really can't help you, Mr Lederer. I found her a job with a chemical export firm but she didn't want it. There are very few jobs in publishing. I've already told you.'

'It's a personal problem. Isobel has a difficulty.'

I said, 'Why don't you let her solve her own problems?'

'Oh, Mrs Hawkins.'

'I've got to go, now.'

'But Isobel apart, can't we meet and talk? And I wish you'd call me Hugh.'

'I'll have to ring you back. What's your number, Mr Lederer?'

He gave me a number and I repeated it slowly enough to make out I was writing it down, which I wasn't.

The Tooleys' house in Lord North Street was one of a row near enough to the Houses of Parliament to contain an old bell for members. It was, in fact, narrower and smaller than Milly's Victorian dwelling. The door was opened by a manservant in such an ordinary brown suit that it seemed to mean to tell you that his employers moved with the times. I was greatly taken by the charm of the interior. I had expected something larger and more imposing: something of a challenge, and here there was none. But there was no time for me to take in more impressions, for a few people were arriving behind me, and when I had left my coat I was waved upstairs where the social noise was going on. Ian Tooley met me on the threshold of the drawing-room and introduced me to his wife, Lady Philippa, and the other guests, and put in my hand the dry sherry I asked for.

Two of the guests already present I knew by name and newspaper pictures: Sir Arthur Cary, the tycoon, who stood somewhat apart, and his vivacious wife who loquaciously held court in a group at the other end of the room.

'Mrs Hawkins was an editor at Ullswater Press,' said Ian Tooley, urging Sir Arthur towards me. 'And now we are so fortunate as to have her with us.'

'Ullswater Press . . .' said Sir Arthur, and gave a gurgle of laughter. 'Well, Martin York certainly took me for a ride.' He continued to laugh so much that I wondered how seriously he had been taken for a ride, and, if it was such a light-hearted matter, why he had caused Martin York to go to prison for seven years.

We sat down fourteen for dinner, in a dining-room with rose-pink walls and a ceiling of a terracotta colour. The pictures were flower paintings in oils, good but not moving, and one portrait of a man, early Victorian, who resembled neither Ian Tooley nor Lady Philippa although he did look like somebody's ancestor. Lady Philippa wore a black lace dress, slightly old-fashioned, remarkably like mine. This made me feel relaxed, it confirmed that I was suitably dressed, and I sensed from her swift sweeping glance that Lady Philippa was mildly amused to find herself dressed virtually the same as another woman in the room.

I sat between one of their cousins, a young man named Aubrey who worked at Sotheby's and a red-faced retired Brigadier General. The candles duly twinkled, the silver glowed and the chatter went on. I made some headway with Aubrey on the subject of *Lucky Jim*, not long published, but when it came to the Brigadier I found him difficult at first. He seemed to glare at me, with watery small eyes, out of his very red face. But his glare was evidently only a mannerism, or perhaps something medical, for although he didn't cease to glare he came round to a conversation when I said something to the effect that he must have had an interesting life.

'Could write a book,' he said.

'Why don't you?'

'Can't concentrate.'

'For concentration,' I said, 'you need a cat. Do you happen to have a cat?'

'Cat? No. No cats. Two dogs. Quite enough.'

So I passed him some very good advice, that if you want to concentrate deeply on some problem, and especially some piece of writing or paper-work, you should acquire a cat. Alone with the cat in the room where you work, I explained, the cat will invariably get up on your desk and settle placidly under the desk-lamp. The light from a lamp, I explained, gives a cat great satisfaction. The cat will settle down and be serene, with a serenity that passes all understanding. And the tranquillity of the cat will gradually come to affect you, sitting there at your desk, so that all the excitable qualities that impede your concentration compose themselves and give your mind back the self-command it has lost. You need not watch the cat all the time. Its presence alone is enough. The effect of a cat on your concentration is remarkable, very mysterious.

The Brigadier listened with deep interest as he ate, his glaring eyes turning back and forth between me and his plate. Then he said, 'Good. Right. I'll go out and get a cat.' (I must tell you here that three years later the Brigadier sent me a copy of his war memoirs, published by Mackintosh & Tooley. On the jacket cover was a picture of himself at his desk with a large alley-cat sitting inscrutably beside the lamp. He had inscribed it 'To Mrs Hawkins, without whose friendly advice these memoirs would never have been written – and thanks for introducing me to Grumpy.' The book itself was exceedingly dull. But I had advised him only that a cat helps concentration, not that the cat writes the book for you.)

While I was talking to my neighbours at dinner, aware of the chatter and tinkle of forks along the rest of the table, I sneaked a glance at the amount everyone else was eating. It seemed enormous in relation to my half. The voices were expressing opinions on the following: numerous people I didn't know; Billy Graham; Senator McCarthy; Colonel Nasser; again, *Lucky Jim*; the Box; and 'They', which meant they, the Government, they, the Americans, they, the Irish, and many other theys; which left a very small world of 'us'; also, Martin York and the shock to his poor father. One young woman took a second helping of a delicious concoction of fruit and frothy cream. She smiled across the table to me, 'I'm eating, for two. Pregnant.' Lady Philippa smiled and said, hastily, 'When are you hoping to finish your lives?' Which curious question, in a moment, resolved its logic by turning out to refer to the *Lives* of two saints which this girl was writing; I learned, too, with the half of my attention that was left over from my neighbours, that although she was only twenty-eight (my age) she already had five children. I assumed she was a Roman Catholic and reckoned that her helpings added up to four times mine. If I hadn't been in conversation with the Brigadier and the young man who worked at Sotheby's I would have advised her that eating for two is not desirable in pregnancy; and I resolved to tell her so later; but as things turned out, after dinner I forgot, being too puzzled and in the disarray of wondering if I had done the wrong thing about something else.

Although I hadn't been to a dinner party as formal and upper-class as this before, I felt quite up to it. I had never considered, in fact, what class I belonged to: I presumed it was Ordinary Class, something like O blood group. I didn't think upper-class habits were so very different from any other English habits. It is true that I had read in novels about such eccentricities as 'the ladies left the men at the table with their port' but I didn't attach these performances to real life. I might as well have been a foreigner. And I will say, now, that I learned a lot about upper-class habits while I was with Mackintosh & Tooley. In the end I concluded it was better to belong to the ordinary class. For the upper class could not live, would disintegrate, without the ordinary class, while the latter can get on very well on its own.

The dinner itself was coming to an end but the chatter went on. At a certain moment there was a hush, not quite a silence. Lady Philippa was looking at me very intensely, and I hadn't the slightest idea why. I supposed she had asked me a question and I looked back enquiringly. Suddenly Lady Philippa got up as if someone had said something that touched her on a tender spot; I thought she was going to make a scene about it. The other women got up, too. But I didn't see what the men had done wrong that the women should leave them like that, haughty and swan-like, sailing out of the room. I would have liked to advise them to pull themselves together. The men shuffled to their feet and looked at me curiously, as if they couldn't believe that I, too, wasn't offended. But, touchy as I was at that hungry period of my life, I perceived nothing to take umbrage about. I, for one, refused to behave rudely just to show solidarity with these oversensitive women, possibly prudes. Lady Philippa murmured, as she passed my chair, 'Are you coming?' But I felt the men had done nothing to deserve such treatment. I was Mrs Hawkins. I sat on.

8

Although I had something to acquire in social savvy, looking back I can now say I wasn't immature in my common sense. In fact, from the time of the dinner party I seemed to perceive that the Tooleys felt more confidence in me, not less, as one might have expected. It was as if they put me into that reliable category of the nanny or the cook who would never let them down. However, my days with Mackintosh & Tooley were numbered; they were numbered to the extent of two more months. I used those two months well.

A large part of an editor's job is rejection. Perhaps nine-tenths. In those days at least, it was not only rejection of manuscripts but of those ideas that seemed to come walking into my office every day in the shape of pensive men and women talking with judicious facial expressions about such mutilated concepts as optimist/pessimist, fascist/communist, extrovert/introvert, highbrow/middlebrow/lowbrow; and this claptrap they applied to art, literature and life to the effect that all joy, wit and the pleasures of curiosity were quite squeezed out.

But along came Emma Loy. She had decided to publish her new novel with Mackintosh & Tooley, who gave a welcoming cocktail party for her in the office boardroom. Along came Emma with her egocentricity, her capriciousness, and her magic and her charm. About so good a writer it seems pointless to say she might have made an excellent actress, but this was a thought her presence evoked.

She had decided to forget her complaints about me to Martin York, and simply presumed that I had decided to forget.

Now, my advice to anyone who knows a person with charm, wit, and talent like Emma, and with some wisdom and intelligence, too, and should fall out with them, is to accept any opportunity of making it up. Because life offers only a few of such people.

And in fact I was genuinely pleased when Emma Loy said, as soon as she saw me at the party, 'Mrs Hawkins, Mrs Hawkins, I can't tell you how relieved I am that you're here. I don't know another soul. I hope you're going to look after my books.'

'Your books look after themselves,' I said.

Which was true. Opinions varied about Emma Loy, but nobody could ever deny that she was a marvellous writer. Ian Tooley had let me read the typescript of her new novel. After the drivel I had been dealing with, Emma's work was a decided relief, it was sheer pleasure, that way of composing a book like a piece of music, that Loy style of ferreting out facts and juxtaposing them with inventions.

I told Emma Loy of my admiration while I eked out my one glass of sherry and she sipped her second. She radiated delight.

I was glad, then, that my quarrel with Emma Loy was over and forgotten. Whether I could trust her or not was beside the point; in fact, I think she didn't believe in friendship and loyalty beyond a certain limit, and maybe she was right; they are ideals that can put too much of a strain on purposes which are perhaps more important. I couldn't see that protecting Hector Bartlett's reputation was much of a purpose, and Emma must have known that he was the *pisseur de copie* that I had called him. But he was her protégé; I imagined the bond between them was sex; and it wasn't till much later that she told me, quite by chance, how he had been useful to her. He had helped her with research and brought her the books she needed. Useful, merely . . . But that explanation was Emma Loy's way of brushing off her own folly. I think she was emotionally lazy, too bound up in her literary activities to form a new relationship or fall in love. She had a morbid dependence on Hector Bartlett even while she knew he was a disaster. Years later he tried to do her a lot of damage.

But now, as was inevitable, Hector Bartlett turned up at the party, and seeing him among the crowd I merely marvelled that Emma could bear to have that *pisseur* breathing down her neck. And I think I wasn't alone in this thought. He made a sort of hole in the crowd as the people he wanted to talk to moved away from him as politely as possible; and Emma, discerning this, went to join him; whereupon the gap closed up again. The people Hector Bartlett hadn't wanted to talk to then hovered warily round the fringe; these were people like myself, including editors and employees from other publishers, literary agents and authors of little fame.

Ian Tooley made his rounds very civilly, explaining here

and there how Mars had passed into the sign of the Fish (or maybe it was that Venus or Mercury had moved into Scorpion), and that, as a consequence, various national problems might be resolved. The ebb and flow of the party soon brought Emma my way again. I remember her getting into an argument with Ian Tooley over his arcane beliefs. It was typical of Emma Loy, and part of her attractiveness, that she ignored all the cocktail-conventions in her conversation. She liked to discuss general subjects. What I heard her say to Ian Tooley on this occasion, or he to her, has largely gone into a flashback blur; except for one clear passage. Ian Tooley said she was a sceptic: 'Don't you even believe in God?'

'Some days I do and some days I don't,' said Emma Loy. 'But one thing I do know – in fact I think it obvious – is that God believes in me.'

That was Emma Loy, and no doubt still is. Standing by Ian Tooley's side at that moment, I gave her my advice that if I were in her place, with my beliefs coming and going some days yes, some days no, I would have a jolly good time the days I believed and repent the days I didn't.

'Mrs Hawkins,' said the famous lady, 'if I take your advice will I become an editor?'

'There's no guarantee about that,' I said.

'Well it's good advice. But I have no matter for repentance.'

Ian Tooley remarked that the study of radionics was taking us beyond good and evil.

Sir Alec Tooley hardly ever appeared. How he arrived at the offices or how he went was a mystery; there must have been some back door exclusive to himself.

About the end of February he called me on the intercom and wearily invited me to come to his office when convenient. I went right away and took his hand, limply held out to me and carelessly withdrawn once the touch had been achieved.

'Mrs Hawkins, we know you are a remarkably reliable woman and so we have decided, after long reflection, to entrust you with a work of criticism which we have decided to publish but which needs a great deal of that application, that scrupulous attention and editing which we believe only you can give.'

My attention was waylaid by the phrase 'remarkably reliable woman' which was almost exactly what Mr Twinny the odd-job man had once said about me to Milly, in my presence. His actual words were, 'Mrs Hawkins is a remarkable reliable woman.' They had been spoken in robust friendship with a good deal of force above the wireless which was chattering in the background.

Sir Alec's utterance and subsequent words of praise were like the cry of a bird in distress, far away across a darkening lake. I had a sense he was offering things abominable to me, like decaffeinated coffee or *coitus interruptus*; and by no means, at that moment, did I want to be a remarkably reliable woman.

'The manuscript', he said, 'needs putting into shape.'

'Do you mean re-writing?' I said.

'Well, of course, that, too. But there are facts to be verified and so on. Grammar and syntax and so forth. Dates.'

My intuition revealed to me there and then that he was talking about a book by the *pisseur de copie* which had been pushed on to them by Emma Loy as part of her price.

'The book,' said Sir Alec, 'is entitled *The Eternal Quest, a study of the Romantic-Humanist Position.* Somewhat deep. It is a comparative study of *The Pilgrim's Progress, Wilhelm Meister* and *Peer Gynt*, or at least, purports to be. I know very little of the subject.'

'I, less,' I said. 'Quite above my head. Who is the author?'

'A Hector Bartlett. He is highly recommended by our Miss Loy.'

I said, 'Oh, don't touch him. He's a *pisseur de copie*. He has no clear ideas. He gets all the facts thoroughly wrong to start with, then he strings them together to form a cooked-up theory.'

'Yes, yes. But what was it you called him in that French designation?'

But I considered Sir Alec's health and well-being unequal to a full explanation. I calmed down. I said I would have a look at the manuscript. I said that, after all, the advice of St Thomas Aquinas had been to rest one's judgement on what is said, not by whom it is said. 'So never mind the author. I'll look at the actual book.'

'We are committed to publish it. A small edition of course. It will involve considerable . . .'

I took the book away; I took it from his hands, so eager to be rid of it, and into mine, which I suddenly felt should be wearing rubber gloves.

I misspent a week in which the book got thoroughly on my nerves. I took it home to read, hoping to be able to concentrate on the incomprehensible pages.

'Perhaps it's above my head,' I said to Milly.

'No fear,' said Milly. 'If you can't understand it, Mrs

Hawkins, it can't be a Christian book.' (By Christian Milly meant human. She would describe the cat as looking at her 'like a Christian'.)

I was suffering from hunger and my diet. The resentment I felt against the book had something in it that I was unable to locate. After all, I could have treated it with the indifference I showed to all the other bad manuscripts that passed through my hands. But this book *The Eternal Quest* was a personal threat. It was Emma Loy who desired it to be put into shape for publication. She knew I was not a fool. But one might as well have taken a carpet-sweeper to clear the jungle as edit that book.

I took it to William Todd, our medical student, always friendly, and in recent weeks, even more friendly towards me. He was an intellectual fellow, accustomed to ideas and the study of them. He brought it back to my room after reading two chapters, the first and the last. 'A lot of balls,' he said. 'Completely phoney. On every page Nietzsche, Aristotle, Goethe, Ibsen, Freud, Jung, Huxley, Kierkegaard, and no grasp whatsoever of any of them. Send it back.'

We had a drink on that.

For the rest of the week I practised what I would say to get out of the job. I practised the speech in my mind and I practised it on Milly. 'What I'm going to say,' I told her, 'is that despite Emma Loy's sponsorship of the work, I myself feel that—'

'Keep that woman's name out of it,' Milly said. 'You know she's dangerous.'

Before the week was out Ian Tooley came to my office with an important expression on his face. I imagined at first he had come to discuss the *Pisseur*'s book.

'How are you, Mrs Hawkins?'

'It's all quite beyond me,' I said. 'I can't possibly cope.'

'Four days of rain on end. I quite agree,' he said. 'But the weather apart, Mrs Hawkins, there is something I want to discuss. Something rather jolly, in fact.'

'It is not jolly,' I said, getting ready for my speech.

'The march of ideas,' he said, settling himself in the chair where my authors generally sat.

He had in fact come to offer me the job of assistant editor of a new quarterly magazine called *The Phantom* which he was founding. It was to publish essays, poems and stories on the supernatural and extra-sensory perception.

There was an upsurge of interest in the supernatural in those years, probably as a result of the uncontemplatable events which had blackened the previous decade.

'Yes,' I said. 'That would be jolly.'

It was jolly, too, that he offered me a rise in pay.

Before he left, he said, 'Are you keeping well, Mrs Hawkins?'

'I'm fine, thank you, Mr Tooley. And you?'

'Oh, I'm all right. It's only that you look different, if I may be personal.'

'Yes, I'm losing weight.'

'Oh, dear. Shall you be thin?'

'No, only normal, I hope.'

'Oh dear. Of course, you could try the Box.'

That was on a Thursday. Friday morning I sent Hector Bartlett's manuscript to Sir Alec with a note, the wording of which I had pondered well: 'I consider that it cannot be improved upon.'

I was looking through some notes about *The Phantom* that Ian Tooley had sent me when the intercom buzzed. It was noon.

The angel of the Lord brought the tidings . . .

'Mrs Hawkins speaking,' I said.

It was Sir Alec. *And she conceived by the Holy Ghost.*

'Mrs Hawkins, if you could see your way to be free at two-thirty this afternoon I should be obliged if you would come and see me here in my office.'

Hail Mary . . . the Word was made flesh.

'Yes, of course, Sir Alec.'

I went to lunch at a pub nearby to eat half a delicious ham sandwich, and drink half a cup of watery coffee and half a glass of port. It was a popular pub for journalists as well as for the people who worked at Mackintosh & Tooley's and publishers in the vicinity of Covent Garden. I was early enough to get a place at a table, but others who came in after me had to stand. The place was soon full of people and noise, the smell of beer, cigarettes and of people. The door swung open and shut as more and more came in. One man had a spaniel on a lead. He let it loose and it ambled round everybody's legs to see what treats it could pick up from friendly customers by way of bits of sandwich or sausage rolls. My eyes followed the dog, for I was going to give it the left-over half of my sandwich if it should come my way. It was at the bar, now, and was nosing a sausage roll which a man was idly letting hang from his left hand while his right hand was holding a glass of beer. Rather comically, the dog just helped himself to a bite of this dangling sausage roll. The man turned and swore at the dog. I now saw who this man was: Hector Bartlett. All in one second, he now took a large dab of mustard from the pot on the counter, dabbed it on the rest of the sausage roll, and gave it to the greedy dog.

'Oh, no,' shouted the few people who had seen this happen, including me. Too late, also, was the dog's master who also had been just in time to witness the nasty work, and to whom the poor beast ran, whining and shaking its head from side to side. I got the barman to give me some water in a deep, clean, glass ashtray. Fortunately, very soon the dog was sick on the floor, and there was a flurry of people with sawdust to mop it up, and a great fussing round the dog. The owner, a young thin man, went over to big Hector Bartlett and said, 'I say, old boy, that was pretty rotten of you.' Which I thought quite a restrained reaction.

But the *Pisseur de copie*, who had obtained a second sausage roll, merely said, in an off-hand way, 'It stole the first half, so I thought it might as well have the second.' The owner of the dog turned away in disgust, fixed the lead on the dog's collar and went out. There was a feeling of relief in the place, for everyone had been expecting a fight.

The *Pisseur*, his chins folded into the collar of his sheepskin coat, his baby-mouth consuming a fresh sausage roll, lolled over the counter, with his eyes on the crowd, and his back to the barman. He was often to be seen in pubs in this neighbourhood at lunch-time and immediately after office hours, hoping to catch the eye of some editor or journalist who could be useful to him. He caught my eye.

'Mrs Hawkins, what a pleasure,' he said, and, with his back still to the barman, turned his head just enough to throw an order for another beer over his shoulder. 'Mrs Hawkins, I understand you're my new editor.'

I didn't reply. I got up and left. It occurred to me on the way to the office that I couldn't stand the publishing scene any longer. Then it occurred to me that this was unfair; the pub was hardly the publishing scene nor was Hector Bartlett representative of it. But there was a residue of uneasiness in my mind about the publishing scene, a weariness of authors, agents, books, printers, binders, critics, editors, when I went in to Sir Alec Tooley's office punctually at half-past two. He hadn't arrived back from lunch yet. I sat down with my thoughts. I was tired of the whole scene and longed to be able to go into a bookshop as in former times and choose a book without being aware of all that went into its making. Besides being weary, I was hungry, but I took pride in that.

Sir Alec arrived all beams and smiles at five past three, ushering before him Emma Loy. I had never seen him in this exuberant mood.

'We have kept you waiting, Mrs Hawkins. Have we kept you waiting?'

He busied himself with Emma's coat and settling her into a chair. They had evidently been to lunch somewhere grand like the Ivy, Rules or the Ritz, and were mellowed with all the wines and rare foods my imagination could impute to the occasion. One of the effects of being on a diet is a kind of puritanical dismay at the idea of other people's eating and drinking, especially the quantity. Three luxurious courses, I thought wildly, as I greeted Emma Loy with my good smile; Rhenish white wine, smoked salmon, then lamb chops with tiny vegetables or something *flambé*, followed by –

The details began to escape my imagination, but anyway my attention was directed quite away from these two and their lunch by the arrival of Ann Clough, the formidable reproach to our national conscience whose maniacal father had been hanged, and who was so nice, and an important director of the firm. She was followed by Colin Shoe who immediately said, 'Emma, you look wonderful,' to the tailored and grey-clad Name who sat back in her armchair, dreamy with lunch. 'Are we late?' said Colin. Clearly this was to be a meeting and it had been called for three o'clock. I thought, paranoically, that I had been called for two-thirty and made to wait in order to put me in my place; but maybe they only forgot to tell me that the time had been changed. Whatever Colin Shoe had been struck off the medical rolls about, it wasn't a lack of bedside manner. He fussed over Emma and exclaimed proudly and justly over her forthcoming novel; and he quite forgot for the moment that the best author was a dead one. Sir Alec had now called someone else on the intercom, in response to which Abigail de Mordell Staines-Knight came in and was introduced to Emma Loy as such.

'I didn't quite catch the name,' said wicked Emma, whereupon Abigail mildly replied, 'Abigail will do.' Abigail had a short-hand notebook. She perched on the edge of a chair on the outskirts of the circle we had formed, with pencil poised.

'This is a very pleasant occasion,' said Sir Alec. 'I doubt if we shall have a great deal of discussion. It is the question of this book by our author Hector Bartlett, entitled *Quest for Eternity* –'

'*The Eternal Quest* I think is the title,' said Ann Clough with a smile at Emma Loy.

'*The Eternal Quest*. There are a few small problems, they

need not detain us for long. Mrs Hawkins, you have under-taken to deal with this book and I have your note that it can't be improved.'

'Exceedingly high praise,' said Colin Shoe, with the opti-mism of one who observes that four months to live is a lifetime.

Abigail squiggled her pencil across the lines of her note-book.

'Mrs Hawkins doesn't want to touch the book,' said Emma Loy. 'You know, Mrs Hawkins, you are terribly prejudiced against Hector.'

'Let us stick to the book,' said Ann, with the tone of a patient schoolteacher. 'We are not here to discuss personali-ties. The book's the thing.'

I spoke directly to Emma Loy. 'Nobody could re-write the book. No-one can edit it. It's awful.'

'I want to do this for Hector,' she said. 'Why are you so down on him?'

'He's a *pisseur de copie*,' I said, and I said it because I could-n't help it. It just came out.

'Oh, God!' said Emma. 'That epithet of yours. It's going the rounds and it's ruining Hector's career. I'm not claiming he's a genius, but –'

'What was that you said, Mrs Hawkins?' said Sir Alec. Colin Shoe looked up at the ceiling.

'*Pisseur de copie*. It means that he pisses hack journalism, it means that he urinates frightful prose.'

'Perhaps we'd better –' said Ann.

'The truth is', said Emma, 'that I'd like to help Hector and I don't know how.' She meant, as I suspected at the time, that she wanted to get him out of her life, and this attempt to get his book published was a valedictory present.

'I'm sure Mrs Hawkins doesn't mean –' said Colin Shoe.

'I am sure that a distinguished author like Miss Loy', said Sir Alec, 'would not recommend an unworthy book, and if I may say so, Mrs Hawkins, your terms of expression are hardly –'

'Not having read the book personally –' said Ann.

Abigail scribbled on, her legs crossed, cool and slim on the edge of her chair.

'I wish you could get to know Hector, Mrs Hawkins,' said Emma. 'He has so many good points.'

It had become almost a private argument between Emma and me. She said Hector Bartlett went to a great deal of trouble over his writing. I told her trouble was the word. 'Agreed,' she said. 'But touch up the book a bit. My dear, what are you here for?' Then I recounted what I had just seen in the pub. 'A great slosh of mustard on a sausage roll,' I said. 'The poor dog.'

'There's another side to Hector,' said Emma. 'After all, how many authors and artists in history have been absolute swine. It's nothing to do with his work. I say you're prejudiced.'

'If you want my advice,' I said to Sir Alec, whose postprandial euphoria I had thoroughly spoiled, 'you will send this book back to the maker, just as a shopkeeper would do with any faulty object, a camera or a tin of beans gone bad. Send it back.'

Poor Ann Clough said, 'Let us be fair –'

'And,' said Emma, 'Mrs Hawkins, your description of the author is obscene.' She turned to Alec. 'You must admit –'

'Miss Loy's name is enough to guarantee –' said Colin Shoe.

'I think we'll have to pass the book to one of our other editors,' said Sir Alec. 'It's a great shame, Mrs Hawkins, but we can't have this. Just when we were counting on you to assist with *The Phantom. The Phantom*', he said, turning to Emma, 'is a new project of ours, a quarterly review of the occult.'

They never published the *Pisseur*'s book. They brought out *The Phantom*, not assisted by me, and it flourished for nearly twenty years.

'It was a pity you had to call him that name,' said Milly that night, when I gave her a replay of the day's events.

'I can't help it. Sometimes the words just come out and I can't stop them. It feels like preaching the gospel.'

'Then you're quite right, Mrs Hawkins. You're quite right to speak out.'

Next day Colin Shoe brought me a month's pay. He said I could leave as soon as I liked, 'to our great regret, Mrs Hawkins.'

I signed for the money and said that I would be leaving almost right away, as soon as I had cleared up a few minor things I had to do. I added, 'And do not forget that Hector Bartlett is a *pisseur de copie*.'

'I won't forget, Mrs Hawkins. None of us will forget. You are looking very smart these days, if I may say so.'

I said good-bye to my colleagues; I sensed a sort of envy in Ann Clough's good-bye, as if I were getting out of something she couldn't. I went to say good-bye to Abigail. Before I left her office, while I was still chatting, I saw, lying sideways on her desk a typed list of about ten names. I looked at them while talking, not really meaning to take them in. One of them was Wanda Podolak.

9

That cold March of 1955 was one of the strangest in my life. Milly Sanders was away all that month in Ireland, where her daughter was ill. I lay long awake at nights, listening to the silence with my outward ears and to a crowding-in of voices with my inward ear.

There was the voice of Martin York, 'Credibility, Mrs Hawkins, credibility is everything. I am attempting to regain credibility for the Press,' and of Ivy, the typist at the Ullswater Press, whose 'n's sounded like 'd's: 'Mr York is id a meeting. It is simply dot possible . . .' Came the shrill short phrases of Patrick's wife, Mabel, thrown at me like stones. 'You, Mrs Hawkins. You, Mrs Hawkins. You sleep with my husband, you make love with him in your bed. You, for your pleasure, Mrs Hawkins . . .' And now Mabel was dead, suddenly in her grave. Her voice was soft on those occasions when her mood swerved, 'Mrs Hawkins, you are so good to us. You have been so kind to Patrick.'

Milly had said, 'You should marry again, Mrs Hawkins.

You're a young woman. Twenty-eight, twenty-nine, is too young to settle for life as a widow.' I had told her part of the story of my brief war-time marriage. 'It was hardly a marriage,' she said. This was objectively true.

During that March after I was pushed out of Mackintosh & Tooley I didn't think of looking for another job. With Milly away, I spent my days taking long rides on the top of buses all over London, to the furthest outskirts and termini. Stanmore, Edgware, Bushey, Chingford, Romford, Harrow, Wanstead, Dagenham, Barking. There were few streets intact although the war had been over ten years. Victorian houses, shops, churches, were separated by large areas of bomb-gap. The rubble had been cleared away, but strange grasses and wild herbs had sprung up where the war-demolished houses had been. While it was still light I rode past the docks and the railway sidings, and the dark pubs not yet open, until it was time to go home again. London was still sooty from coal fires in those days. Wembley, Hackney, Islington, Southall, Acton, Ealing. And sometimes I walked round the City, soon to be reconstructed with eloquent, rich high-rises. Sometimes I went to Richmond, to Greenwich, to Dulwich, Hampton and Kew where I walked in the vast lonely parks on dry days and was solicited at times by men in raincoats whom I thoroughly scared off. Surbiton, Ewell, Croydon and as far as Orpington. So I spent my days after days on the top of the buses staring out of the window and watching with discreet eyes my fellow passengers, most of them shabby, and, if they were not alone, listening with half an ear to their talk, mostly about their families and friends, their shopping and their jobs; and not once in all those long rides did I hear a snatch of conversation about a general topic.

At times I felt faces looming over me. The conductor, the passengers as they passed to get on or off, shrill schoolchildren and burly mothers who had been unable to find a seat on the lower deck. I felt like Lucy Snowe in *Villette*, who walked, solitary in Brussels on a summer night, among the festival crowds; the faces pressing round her, of people made hilarious by the occasion, were made even more grotesque by her state of hallucination induced by laudanum.

There was no such hectic celebration in sober London but I experienced a throb and a choking of hysteria in the London voices around me and in the bland and pasty, the long and dour, the pretty and painted faces of the people. Barnet, Loughton, Hendon, Northolt, Willesden, Camberwell, Plumstead, Kingston, Bromley. I had lunches in noisy pubs, leaving half on my plate, to the consternation of many barmaids whose eyes seemed to me too wild, their lips too red to be real. I had tea and half a bun in tea-shops where no waitress cared what I didn't eat. I was tempted to reflect that my diet had the same effect as a drug, but I put the thought from me. I thought about my life as Mrs Hawkins and came to no conclusion whatsoever. 'Good evening, Mrs Hawkins,' said our next-door neighbour's new wife, as I turned in our gate at Church End Villas at the same time as she turned in hers.

I was married in 1944 at the age of eighteen to Tom Hawkins. I met him in July and married him on the 28th August for which purpose he got special leave from the army. Tom was a parachutist, a sergeant in the airborne troops. I had not long left school and had joined the Land Army. It was as a land-girl that I first met Tom. He was home on leave at the estate where I worked. I was a great, robust girl but not truly fat as I had been lately. Tom was a tall fellow, with a long thin face very dark of complexion; he was one of those dark Englishmen that make you wonder where the darkness came from – the Romans? the wrecked mariners of the Spanish Armada? maybe a Norman import from the remnants of the Gallic mercenaries? He was now twenty-four and had been attending an agricultural college when the war broke out.

Tom's father had some land in Hertfordshire. It was settled that Tom would be a farmer when the war was over, and I would be a farmer's wife. I wonder what sort of farmer's wife I would have made if Tom had lived? I had chosen to go into the Land Army because I was big and strong, and because, after my years at school, the idea of being out in the open in all weathers was one of freedom as opposed to the office work I would otherwise have been sent to do in those war years of total recruitment for all under the age of forty-five. But I had a bookish side, which Tom didn't live to see.

I had met Tom Hawkins at a dance, then we met again. Then, when he went back to his unit, we wrote to each other, at first every week, then twice a week, then every day. He phoned me when he could. I had no knowledge of where he was stationed; it was secret like everything else of interest at that time; his letters had to be addressed to a number, a division and some other rigmarole ending with HM Forces. Tom came on leave again, for a weekend, and asked me to marry him. I thought it over for a fortnight, but the interval was only a formality. For at this stage I was absolutely in love, as much in love as Tom. My parents, Tom's father and sister, and two of my school friends who were on the land with me, came to my wedding on the 28th of August. I wore my school-concert dress, long and white, which did very well, and saved clothing coupons. Tom wore his uniform. We had four days in London, in a borrowed flat. We had intended to go to theatres, but we never did. We were disturbed only by a few incendiary bombs and V1s, for which there were air-raid warnings. The V2s for which there were no warnings had not started. We went to Hampton Court and to Kew. We walked in Hyde Park, round the Serpentine, almost every day, and on to Kensington Gardens, and to tea with chocolate cake at Gunter's in Curzon Street at the extravagant price of two shillings and sixpence each, plus tip.

After that I was a land-girl again, looking out for my letters addressed to Mrs Hawkins. I knew Tom would soon have to go into action on the Western front where the Germans were toughly holding out. To steel myself and prepare for the worst, in those weeks since our wedding, I used to secretly rehearse a telegram from the War Office advising me that my husband had been killed in action. The personnel officer in our group would say, 'There's a telegram for you, Mrs Hawkins.' And that would be that. 'Is there anything you would like, won't you lie down? You must be very brave, Mrs Hawkins. You aren't the only one . . .'

Tom put in an unexpected appearance on Monday night, 11th September. He was to go back next day. We took a tiny room at the local pub. Tom didn't say so, but I guessed he was AWOL, as we called 'Absent without leave'. We were Mr and Mrs Hawkins. I supposed he was going into battle very soon. What a fool he had been, I thought, to join the parachuters.

After supper downstairs he left me and I went up to bed; he

had said he felt he could do with a drink. He had already drunk three double whiskies. They happened to have whisky that night in the pub. It was a special consignment. Whisky was scarce at that time. I was in bed by nine, reading a book and waiting for Tom. There was a considerable noise downstairs in the public bar, but I had fallen asleep by closing time, when Tom woke me up, bursting into the room wild and drunk.

Now, it is my advice to anyone getting married, that they should first see the other partner when drunk. Especially a man. Drink can mellow, it can sweeten. Too much can make a person silly. Or it can make them savage: this was the case with Tom. I hadn't seen him drunk before. He broke up the place, starting with the china ewer and basin on the washstand and ending with the wall-mirror. I was on my feet and had tried to stop him when he heaved the mattress off the bed and tried to push it out of the window. This only had the effect of his hurling me across the room, after which the mattress went out of the window. And all the time swearing and shouting, while the landlord and his wife, first standing in the doorway, then called their son to fetch the police.

Tom made off, back to his camp, without even looking at me before the policeman arrived; I don't know how he got transport; probably he got a lift. I helped to put things straight in the room, with the landlady puffing and clucking; I settled the bill for damage, and went back to my billet in the big old house where we were quartered. The policeman was kindly in the circumstances.

I wonder if my marriage would have lasted? I thought, even then in my inexperience, that this couldn't be Tom Hawkins' normal behaviour. It must be war-nerves, or something like that. But then, I thought, Tom was one of thousands, he wasn't the only one. I think, now, that if I had shown the strong side of my character right from the start, Tom wouldn't have broken out like that. I had a great bruise on my forehead where it had struck the wall, and others on my arms. I had a cut on my neck. It is my advice to any woman getting married to start, not as you mean to go on, but worse, tougher, than you mean to go on. Then you can slowly relax and it comes as a pleasant surprise. I hadn't shown Tom my strength, and perhaps this also included my bookishness; I had been wifely, docile, in love, during those brief days, and Tom didn't know me at all.

I had no letter from Tom for eleven days. But in fact he was killed six days later, at Arnhem in Holland, where the Allied airborne troops had landed and were surrounded. I never knew if Tom was killed in the air while landing, or if he managed to reach the ground to fight. Tom's letter, eleven days later, came the day after the telegram. There had been some delay in the handing over of Tom's identification by the Germans to the Red Cross.

We were having a lecture in the great hall on the subject of cattle-breeding. I was called out. 'Now look, my dear, there's a wire for you . . .' And the next day in the ordinary post, Tom's letter, a short one, written before he had left England. He made no reference at all to his wild outbreak. Had he remembered it? Had he thought, perhaps, it was of no account, just one of those things in married life? I will never know. His letter gave no hint. It was a love letter.

10

The printer's shop in Notting Hill Gate where Cathy the book-keeper had gone to work after the Ullswater Press had closed down was on my bus route one afternoon. I decided to look in on Cathy. Mr Wells asked me to sit down on a chair in the noisy outer workshop while he went to tell Cathy. 'I don't want to interrupt . . .' I said.

'No interruption, ma'am. Aren't you the lady who recommended Cathy? I seem to remember . . .'

'Yes, I came with her for her interview.'

'You must be Mrs Hawkins, of the Ullswater Press.'

'The late Ullswater Press,' I said.

'Yes, a sad affair. I must say, Mrs Hawkins, you're looking very well.'

'Thank you, Mr Wells. I hope everything's fine with you?'

'Everything's fine. And I must say, Mrs Hawkins, if you'll pardon my saying so you look ten years younger than the last time I saw you.'

I was twenty-nine. This meant I must have looked ten years older the first time.

Mr Wells was a grey-haired bespectacled man with a wrinkled face, long nose and a generally Dickensian appearance. None the less his words cheered me up so considerably that I realized then and there how depressed I had been, riding about the faceless streets and shabby suburbs of London on the tops of buses, for the best part of a month.

'Thank you, Mr Wells.'

Cathy came beaming with that smile of gratitude beyond what was called for. Above the din Cathy cackled her delight at my visit; her eyes were fixed on me behind her extra-thick lenses. It was impossible to talk through the noise but it was near closing-time, so I waited for her to get ready and took her to supper at a newly opened French restaurant in the Bayswater Road. We were ushered to a discreet corner, out of the way of the more glamorous clients. I didn't in the least resent this, and Cathy, excited at our meeting, didn't notice. And, in fact, I dwelt with part of my thoughts, while Cathy cackled with her terrible voice and often unintelligible English, on the desire that had been taking hold of me all this month of March, to have a more attractive life; I needed some compelling charm.

I forgot about glamour and turned my attention fully on Cathy when she said, 'Do you remember that red-head man, he would stop you in the Park, he would want that his books can be published by Mr York, that he should give you so much trouble?'

'Hector Bartlett,' I said.

'Is the name,' said Cathy. 'He come now these days by Mr

Wells to get printing done and I say to Mr Wells you mind he don't pay, that man.'

I imagined that the *Pisseur* was arranging to have some of his work privately printed, since he was unable to get a publisher. But on carefully and warily catechizing Cathy throughout the meal I managed to gather that his printing commission was a very special case, almost a challenge to Mr Wells. It consisted in 'printing in columns like in a newspaper', and on paper like a newspaper, so that the final result would look like a cutting from an actual newspaper.

I was quite puzzled. 'Does he have it copied from an actual newspaper?' I said in one of my cross-questions.

'No, no. He bring a page, it is typed out. It must be made like from the newspaper.'

'What does he want that for? Any idea?'

'To Mr Wells he says it is the new form of fiction. Mr Wells thinks he's crazy but OK, no rude words, I print it and he pays.'

That was all I could get out of Cathy. That I had lost my job through refusing to promote the *Pisseur* I thought well to keep to myself.

'Why you don't eat, Mrs Hawkins? Half you leave on your plate,' said Cathy.

Young Isobel Lederer was still at No. 14 Church End Villas, in her third month of pregnancy. At first she had confided in Kate because she was a nurse, then in William because he was a medical student, then in the Carlins because they were a married couple, and about the same time that she informed her Daddy she confided in me because I was Mrs Hawkins.

We felt that Milly, who was in any case away in Ireland,

need not be troubled by the news at this point. Nor did Wanda share the secret, with her panic morals and her hysterical troubles. Isobel, having told five people about her pregnancy, carried on uncaring, as if it was our problem not hers. In a way she was right, because her first suggestion had been that she should procure an abortion. This was not an easy, legal course of action in those years, but her Daddy and money could have arranged it. Isobel had gone to Kate and William with this idea in mind. They had counselled strongly against it. Isobel consulted others. Basil Carlin had wavered but his wife Eva would have none of it. Finally Hugh Lederer declared himself dead against it, and I opposed it so strongly on the grounds of danger, immorality and guts-repugnance, that she gave up the idea, and her pregnancy now became our problem. Hugh Lederer, in fact, tried to reduce it to his problem and mine. To this end he proposed marriage to me. 'It would be good for Isobel to have a mother,' said this amazing fellow.

I could have said that it would be good for her to have a husband; and I could have added that, at the age of twenty-nine, I wasn't minded to take on a girl of twenty-two as a daughter and become a grandmother as well; I could have told him that I wasn't anywhere near in love with him; but all I said was No. And it is my advice, when you have to refuse any request that admits of no argument, you should never give reasons or set out your objections; to do so leads to counter-reasons and counter-objections. So to Hugh Lederer I said No.

There was no way of knowing whether it would be good for Isobel to have a husband, presumably the father of the child, for she was vague when the possibility of her marrying the father was proposed to her.

'Do you love the man?' said Eva Carlin.

'I don't know.'

As it happened she didn't know quite who the father was. And in the third month of her pregnancy, between her bouts of morning sickness when she stayed home from her job, and those evenings when she had no dinner-dates or outlets for her high spirits, having gained our attention she gradually let it be known that there were three claimants for fatherhood, none of whom she thought good enough to marry.

Hugh Lederer got Kate to call a meeting at the house. He mounted the stairs with a heavy and weary tread as if it were he who was carrying the baby. The meeting was held in the Carlins' bed-sitting-room, on account of its being the largest.

But this was a mistake: it was next door to Wanda's room. She was not in the secret and was naturally curious about the evening party at the Carlins, who normally kept themselves so very much to themselves. William clattered in after me; Wanda was at her door to watch. Kate arrived with a note-book in her hand; Wanda took this opportunity of going to the bathroom. I suppose I made matters worse by coming out on the landing while Wanda's activities were going on, calling up to Isobel that we were ready and would she bring three more glasses. Wanda retreated, slamming her door, very offended at being excluded. I noticed this with only part of my attention because the business on hand was uppermost, and then came the question of coffee cups and the bottle of sherry, the bottle of port, the glasses; and were there enough chairs, would we sit on the divan beds? And it was so strange to see the Carlins' room for the first time, what it was like, with their little kitchen adjoining, that nobody gave much thought to Wanda. With Isobel, who arrived with a tinkle of glasses and another bottle of something in her hands, we were seven. But we managed to sound like twenty. Hugh, William and Basil Carlin filled the room with their voices, making the most noise, but Kate was interrupting with her expert knowledge of what facilities and benefits were available to Isobel under the National Health scheme.

'Isobel', said the father, 'has no need of the National Health with its homes for fallen women. I can buy her a small flat, then if she gets a decent job, say, in publishing –'

'Why don't you take her home to live with you?' said Eva Carlin coming out of her kitchen carrying a plate of fanciful snacks, with that way she had of walking with her elbows out as one who means business.

We had all sat down and Basil Carlin was helping his wife to serve the drinks and snacks.

'Live with Daddy?' said Isobel. 'No, I don't like Sussex. I like London.'

'Isobel', said Hugh, 'likes artists and so on. She likes culture.'

'What a life for a baby!' said Kate. 'Those cultural groups don't know what hygiene is, they don't even know what clean is. I remember I was sent to an arty house in Holland Park –'

'Maybe we should get down to business,' William said. Isobel, looking very pretty, with a rosy flushed face and her fair hair short and shiny, sat next to him.

'I appreciate very much you all being here,' said Hugh. 'I

appreciate that you want to stand by Isobel and that there's no prudery involved.'

'Have you seen *The Teahouse of the August Moon?*' asked Isobel of William.

'No, I don't go to the theatre. What's that got to do with it?'

'Nothing. I was only wondering, in case you'd been, what you thought of it. You should see *Antonio's Spanish Ballet*, it's on at –'

'And if I get her a flat, she could get someone to look after the baby –'

'Wouldn't you want her to marry the father of the child?' said Basil Carlin.

'That's what I say,' said Eva. 'Make the swine marry her, whoever he is.'

'*Salad Days*,' Isobel confided to William, 'was pretty good. I haven't been to *Wonderful Town* yet, the bookings –'

'Come on, Isobel,' said William. 'Tell us who the father is. That's what we all want to know.'

'Yes, tell us that,' said Hugh. Why he had not already asked her this in private I could not understand. But I have sometimes observed that people close to one another can discuss their private affairs before others better than alone. Hugh Lederer evidently assumed there was only one possible man. 'It would be a help,' he said, 'if you could indicate who he is.'

Isobel treated this as if it were a guessing-game at a party, handing out the clue: 'Oh, it's one of those boys in Fleet Street or in publishing. You know how they promise to get you a job in publishing, and you sleep with them, and then they don't know of any jobs in publishing and to be quite fair, it isn't easy to get a job in publishing. Daddy doesn't realize that.'

'Do you mean to say that these men don't take precautions?' said Basil Carlin, very shocked.

'You can't ask my daughter to go into details,' said Hugh.

I remembered then what Hugh Lederer had told me on that occasion at the Savoy: Hector Bartlett was one of Isobel's friends who was trying to get her a job in publishing. I was so horrified at the idea that he might be the father of Isobel's baby that I swallowed the whole of my sherry instead of leaving half. I said, 'Don't tell me it's Hector Bartlett?'

'No,' said Isobel. 'It can't be him, but he likes to think he's the father. I only slept with him once because he offered me a job with a publisher. But that was too long ago for him to be the father. He would marry me and make out he's the father; he's been hanging around here for months.'

I registered these last words without their making an impression. It is frequently the case that we lose important parts of what people say in our predominant interest in the other parts. All I noticed at the time was that the *pisseur* wanted to marry Isobel. I overlooked 'he's been hanging around here for months'.

'You couldn't possibly marry that man,' I said.

'I wouldn't marry any of them,' said Isobel.

'Fair enough,' said Hugh.

'What a life for a baby!' said Kate. 'You should have it adopted. It needs a respectable home.'

I said the idea of giving away a baby was too sad to be contemplated, especially when there was no material hardship involved. Isobel agreed: 'I don't see why I should go to a lot of trouble and then have nothing to show for it.'

Kate offered to look for a flat for Isobel. William wrote down the name of a gynaecologist. Eva Carlin agreed, on thinking it over, that Isobel shouldn't marry a man she wasn't in love with. Basil Carlin in a grave voice implored Hugh Lederer to persuade his daughter to go straight from now on. I agreed to be the godmother. Isobel said she hadn't been to see *A Star is Born*, was it any good? Hugh Lederer said he appreciated very much our solidarity with Isobel, which he hoped would continue. The meeting was over. Everyone left in a friendly spirit. 'You'll make a great godmother, Mrs Hawkins,' said Hugh.

Wanda caught me on the landing just as I was about to go up to my room.

'Mrs Hawkins, Mrs Hawkins.'

My mind was still occupied with the fuss and hubbub of the meeting, the sherry and snacks, Isobel and her problem and her doting parent. I half expected Wanda to ask me, as she stood repeating my name on the landing outside her room, if I could get her a job in publishing.

'Yes, Wanda, do you want me?'

'Mrs Hawkins, you must speak with me. You must come into my room.' She stood bobbing her body forward with every phrase, in great earnest. She looked to right and left, then hastily backed into her room, beckoning.

'You plot, Mrs Hawkins,' said Wanda. 'You are all day away from the house. Don't tell me you go to a job because I know you have lost your job. You leave the house to go to those people and you come now in the evening with the other tenants here, to ruin my name. You plot against me. My Box – I make no money from it. I do it for a favour. I help the sick.'

Wanda's Box was open and visible. She had a little pile of cards and a printed booklet open at a page which seemed to have some tabular arrangement. But this was all I could see at a glance. I wasn't about to answer Wanda's accusations of a plot. I just stood and looked at her. The more I heard of the Box, the more I was convinced, as I still am, that it was a lot of rubbish. But was it any more mad than my compulsive Hail Marys at twelve o'clock noon? I went on standing, looking at poor Wanda, in a dreadful state as she was. I decided then and there to give up those Hail Marys; my religion in fact went beyond those Hail Marys which had become merely a superstition to me.

'Mrs Hawkins, you are making a plot against me in the house. Is it my fault you are ill? You are getting thin, you are wasting, wasting, and you will die.'

'Wanda, I'm feeling fine. Why don't you talk to a priest? You should see a priest,' I said. 'In the morning I'll ring Father Stanislas –'

She interrupted with a wild cry, one of her long wails, as if the mention of the Polish priest had inflicted a physical wound. Father Stanislas was a small, mild, bespectacled, white-haired man who was known in the house through having visited Wanda several times about a year before, when she was ill in bed. Wanda now sat on the bed and screamed. I withdrew rapidly. I was suddenly unable to cope without Milly in the house. The Carlins opened their door.

'She's having one of her fits,' I said.

'Another letter?'

'No, I don't think so. I think she's having a breakdown, and I can't make head or tail of what she's saying.'

Wanda was now quiet in her room. Eva Carlin knocked at the door. 'Wanda,' she said, 'would you like a cup of tea?'

Wanda opened her door. 'Go,' she said. 'Go and plot that I am mad. That you report me to the priest. That you decide that my friends and my sister should turn against me. Is it my fault that Mrs Hawkins is to die?'

'I'll bring you a cup of tea,' said Eva Carlin.

I went upstairs. Kate and William were looking over the banisters. 'What's going on?'

'I don't know. She needs a sedative – have you got one, Kate?'

'Yes, but I won't administer it without a doctor's prescription.'

'I will,' said William.

But Wanda wouldn't open her door again to anyone. William came up, after his efforts to persuade her, and knocked on my door. 'Can I come in?'

We sat and talked about Wanda for a while. I told him of her mystifying predictions about my wasting away and dying. 'I feel a bit spooky,' I said.

'She needs professional treatment,' said William. 'And the reason you feel spooky, Mrs Hawkins, is that you don't have a sex life. At your age you're bound to feel spooky without sex.'

I was pulling myself together from this species of shock-treatment, when he added, 'By the way, were you christened "Mrs Hawkins", Mrs Hawkins?'

'No,' I said, 'I was christened Agnes. But I'm called Nancy.'

So I spent the night with William on my threequarter-sized bed, with my mind free of everything but ourselves.

1 1

My advice to any woman who earns the reputation of being capable, is to not demonstrate her ability too much. You give advice; you say, do this, do that, I think I've got you a job, don't worry, leave it to me. All that, and in the end you feel spooky, empty, haunted. And if you then want to wriggle out of so much responsibility, the people around you are outraged. You have stepped out of your role. It makes them furious.

I often wonder what would have happened to my life if William had not been a tenant on the top floor of 14 Church End Villas, South Kensington, that rooming-house, shabby but clean, that to-day is a smart and expensive set of flats, gutted and restructured, far beyond the means of medical students, nurses, and the likes of us as we were.

It was the next morning, at nine-thirty after William had gone off to his lectures, that the telephone rang downstairs. I went down the two flights in my dressing-gown to answer. Usually, I was up and dressed by eight o'clock, but this morning was different. Emma Loy was on the line, with her magic and her way of overlooking her own past offences. 'Mrs Hawkins, I want your help,' she said, as if she wasn't really responsible for my losing two jobs.

'I'm afraid, Miss Loy –'

'Call me Emma, for goodness sake.'

'I can't be of much help to anyone at the present time.'

'But, Mrs Hawkins, you are a tower of strength, I say it in quotes of course.'

'What's the problem, Emma,' I said.

'Well, could we meet and talk?'

'Do you know of a job for me?' I said. 'A job in publishing?'

'Mrs Hawkins, I think you've misunderstood the situation. I honestly didn't want you to leave Mac'n Tooley. On the other hand, believe me, my dear, between ourselves, you're well out of it. Will you lunch with me at the Ivy?'

'To-day?'

'To-day.'

'I'm afraid I can't.'

'Oh, can't you?'

'No, I'm lunching with my boyfriend.'

This was true. I had a date with William at the ABC in Old Brompton Road.

'Mrs Hawkins,' said Emma, 'I understand your state of mind. I'm not a novelist for nothing. If you would only let me explain. I myself am in great difficulties. And I personally would greatly appreciate your giving me an hour, a half-hour, of your time which I genuinely appreciate is very . . .'

I agreed to meet her at six at Grosvenor House in Park Lane. It is useless to conceal the fact that I looked forward to the meeting with the usual excitement that Emma managed universally to invoke. Although many people deplored her I never met anyone who would willingly miss a date with her.

I had no sooner put down the phone than Wanda came down the stairs. 'Who was that, Mrs Hawkins?'

'A friend of mine.' I think my voice was harsh. Certainly I was afraid of psychic contagion. Wanda was no longer as she used to be, amiably receiving her ladies, those clients who used to call for fittings or with alterations to be done. It seemed to me there were very few customers for Wanda these days.

'You spoke to Father Stanislas. I heard you.'

My fear was irrational but strong. I must have appeared guilty; probably I backed away from her.

'No, Wanda. You need to see a doctor.'

'What! You have talked to my enemies that say I am mad. You plot. All in this house are plotting to take me away by a doctor.'

'Why don't you see Father Stanislas first?'

She ran upstairs to her room, wailing.

I sat with William in the ABC while he ate his sandwich and the spare half of mine. I was absolutely at ease with William, and always have been.

'Wanda's in a bad way again this morning,' I said. 'She thinks we are all plotting against her.'

'With the result', said William, 'that we'll have to sort of plot against her. At least she should see a doctor.'

'Or a priest. There's a Father Stanislas, one of the Polish community.'

'Get him to come and see her,' said William, 'and then forget her. You take on too much. Leave something for the specialists.'

'I'd like to make some arrangement for Wanda before Milly comes home. I'm thinking of Milly,' I said.

'We should do something about ourselves before Milly returns,' said William.

'What should we do?'

'Take a flat. A small flat, and share.'

It seemed to me the clear and obvious thing to do, so evident that I was surprised there were no complications. I was accustomed to obstacles. I said, 'Aren't we being a bit precipitate?'

'Nancy, do you think so, yourself?'

'Not if I find a job.'

'Then look for a flat. Fairly quiet for my studies. You're a capable woman, Mrs Hawkins.'

'I'm getting a bit tired of being capable.'

'I know,' he said. 'Don't take on unnecessary responsibilities, and simply abandon anything you've taken on, except me. That's my advice. You're looking lovely.'

'I went to the hairdresser,' I said.

That afternoon I went to Brompton Oratory, and after many enquiries which involved waiting about and being passed from hand to hand, priest to priest, I finally obtained a telephone number for Father Stanislas. Something about this search wore me out so much that I couldn't make the last effort to ring him up. I remembered a story I was told by a man who was invited to dinner in a provincial city at the home of a girl he was in love with, a nervously important occasion for him. It was a rainy night. He couldn't find the house, having first mistaken Aldington Way for Aldington Gardens, then having tried 'Street', 'Avenue', 'Crescent' and 'Terrace', up and down both ways; finally, after stopping people to enquire, and being misdirected, looking into fruit and tobacconist shops with his problem, and tramping around, approached 10A Aldington Way, which he knew was certainly the right house at last, with the name on the door and the light on behind the curtains. But he didn't ring the doorbell. He walked away and on, past the house, and never saw the girl again.

With me, too, the last lap was just too much. With Father Stanislas's number on a slip of paper in my handbag, I made my way early to Grosvenor House. I spent some time making myself presentable in the ladies' room, then came out to Emma Loy.

Grosvenor House was not my idea of the best place for a serious talk. There were too many smart and scented people about, girls and women with furs and A-line dresses or black box-coats and skirts, men too carefully dressed, some with over-padded shoulders, obvious spivs, as we then called the post-war crooks. In that ambience of spivs and their molls, one elderly couple, newly arrived with their battered leather bags from the country, wearing their shapeless country things with raincoats over their arms, looked furtively around, totally bewildered by this brave new world. The porters ushered them out of sight as Emma Loy appeared, handsome in her swinging fur coat, her smart grey dress and pearls.

'Mrs Hawkins, how nice you look with your hair done like that. And you've lost weight, it suits you.'

'You look nice, too.'

We ordered gins and tonic. 'What amazing people,' said Emma, looking round. She had been quick to see that her choice of meeting-place was a mistake. 'I think we should have met somewhere quieter.'

'But the scene is amusing,' I said. 'Quite new to me.'

'And to me,' she said. 'I suppose, as a novelist, I should welcome any experience. Of course, a novelist doesn't really have to undergo every experience, a glimpse is enough.'

I felt, almost, as if it was I, not she, who had chosen the place. But she, quick to thought-read, added, 'I should have picked a more suitable spot. But let's make the best of it.'

Our drinks were served, and Emma nibbled a peanut. Then she said, 'Mrs Hawkins, why do you hate Hector Bartlett?'

'Oh, don't worry,' I said. 'He's got nothing to do with me. I've got nothing to do with him. I'm out of publishing, now. He only wants to use people.'

'Now, if it's a job in publishing you want, you can, I think, count on me. Not right away of course, but eventually. I want to talk about Hector. He's very, very hurt by you, Mrs Hawkins. I think it all began one morning last summer . . .' said the novelist, 'and he met you in the park on the way to your office. Hector was delighted. It was a lovely day in the park, Green Park, I think, or St James's, one or the other . . . He admired you so much, caring as you do for everybody. Then suddenly, without warning you turned on him with that deadly appellation.' Emma lowered her voice: '*Pisseur de copie*. Do you know what that means to a writer, how it affects him? Look at it from the human point of view.'

I was fascinated by her rhetoric. It was a new side of Emma Loy. She was saying things she wouldn't dream of writing or putting her name to. Her tone was not that usually associated with Emma Loy. This meaningless coinage, 'look at it from a human point of view', as if I were another species, must either be put on for my benefit, in which case she had miscalculated my intelligence, or she herself was under some emotional strain; and I had noticed before, once or twice in my job, that the most intelligent and sophisticated of writers are often banal and incoherent under an emotional pressure of real life. I decided to sip my gin and tonic and let her continue.

'You see,' she said, 'I'm leaving next week for the United States where I'll stay for some time, I think. My books are doing rather well over there. And before I leave, I do want to make things all right between Hector and you. How can I go away with an easy mind if you put it about every time you get a job in publishing that he's a (lowered voice) *pisseur de copie?* It's a very hurtful term. And it's not at all like you, Mrs Hawkins.'

I was myself putting on an air while Emma Loy was speaking; it suggested that I was only partly attending to what she was saying. I was assisted by the fact that a more elegant clientèle had begun to replace the lurid six-o'clock set. People were arriving in evening dress in small groups, young and middle-aged, mainly handsome, all very happy.

I turned my gaze from the passing scene to Emma Loy, and I said, 'Any better phrase that you can honestly suggest might apply, I'll be willing to give it careful consideration.'

'Aren't you being rather hard?'

'You must be relieved to be getting rid of him, Miss Loy.'

'Please call me Emma. I know that you stick to Mrs Hawkins and it suits you. It's a matter of your own preferences. I don't at all want to get rid of Hector. In fact I shall miss him very much while I'm in America. Do you realize how dedicated he is to my work? He knows all my works by heart. He can quote chapter and verse, any of my novels. It's amazing.'

'Does he quote it right?'

'No. He generally gets it wrong, I'll admit. But his dedication to me is there. But that's by the way. I was hoping to appeal to you on a personal level.'

'What a marvellous colour, that orange chiffon dress, see, on that girl over there,' I said.

Emma had to admit it was a glorious colour. She let a silence fall for a moment.

Then, 'Hate can turn to love,' she said.

I gave this a moment's thought. 'Maybe on the Continent,' I said, 'or Latin America. But you know very well, Miss Loy, that here in England love and hate are two entirely different things. They are not even opposites. According to my outlook, love comes in the first place from the heart and hate arises basically from principle.'

'You're being very insular,' she said. But I think, from her tone, she realized at this point that her mode of argument had been badly chosen. Anyway, I said, no doubt I was insular, not surprising since I had been born and brought up on an island. Then I looked round at the evening-dress scene. 'I'm dazzled by all this, I must say,' I said; and I started to gather up my bag and gloves as if to go.

'We're getting away from the point,' said Emma. 'You know, Mrs Hawkins, time goes on, and you must think of your future. You don't want to be a lonely woman all your life.'

I sat back again in my chair and told her that she had no hope whatsoever of getting rid of Hector Bartlett on to me.

'And if he ever comes my way again, should I get another job as an editor, I'll still put him down as a *pisseur de copie*.'

'It's slanderous, he could sue,' said Emma.

'Let him sue. It's fair comment.'

'Well he's bound to come your way again, not necessarily in publishing. You know, I only want to see Hector settled before I leave for the US. And I'm surprised if you mean to imply that you haven't seen him around. He spends a lot of time with that woman in your house at Church End Villas. You must have seen him come and go, and know what's going on.'

In fact, I didn't spend so very much time in the house. I was out all day, and if I wasn't out in the evening I would mostly be in my top-floor room or in the kitchen with Milly. I imagined Emma was referring to Isobel's past relations with Hector Bartlett, but I doubted she had entertained him in her room. The only comings and goings in the house had been people visiting Wanda, although lately she had fewer visitors; they no longer crowded the landing outside the room, waiting while she made her fittings. I hadn't noticed any comings and goings at all for Isobel. She obviously carried on her affairs elsewhere.

'No,' I said to Emma. 'The girl only knows him casually.'

'What girl?' said Emma in a way that made me cautious.

'A girl who lives in the house. She knows Hector Bartlett, but it's only a casual friendship.'

'Oh, you mean the one who's expecting a baby and wants to pin it on to Hector?'

'To my knowledge, she doesn't want to pin it on to anyone, especially not him.'

'That's not how I heard it, really, Mrs Hawkins.'

'God knows what you've heard, Miss Loy. I don't think it's our business, anyway.'

'But I wasn't discussing the girl,' said Emma.

'I thought you were.'

'No,' said Emma. 'It's a woman he met last spring. He met her through the girl, that's true. He obtained a dinner suit second-hand, poor fellow, for some occasion and had to have it altered. The woman is a dressmaker, don't tell me you don't know. As a novelist, I find the story enthralling, of course, Mrs Hawkins. There are no end of subtleties and interpretations involved.'

I could see Emma Loy was genuinely enthusiastic about the story element. I could never resist feeling flattered when she spoke to me 'as a novelist', for she usually reserved that side of herself for other writers on her own level, or those hand-picked interviewers whom she occasionally agreed to talk to.

'The possibilities are numerous and extremely fascinating,' mused Emma. 'It's been going on since last spring.'

'You must mean Wanda Podolak,' I said. 'I had no idea she knew Hector Bartlett.' I gathered up my gloves again. 'Well, I wish her well of him, whatever the subtle possibilities. I hardly think he has much to do with Wanda. She's a poor woman, not very strong. And I don't think he would take up with anyone, far less a poor dressmaker, who couldn't be of the slightest use to him.'

I now had it fixed in my thoughts that Emma was somehow trying to make me jealous, and was obscurely promoting the desirability of Hector Bartlett. Emma wanted to get rid of him.

'Must you really go? We could go somewhere nice for a bite,' said Emma.

I thanked her but said I had to go. On the way to the door Emma said, 'I haven't really explained the whole situation. You must think I'm being very mysterious.'

'You want to get rid of Hector Bartlett on to me,' I said.

'Not necessarily on to you,' she said. 'But it would be a solution. You have to stop using that nomenclature.'

'What nonsense,' I said.

'Can I drop you in a taxi?'

'No thanks, I'm going to walk.'

Out in the street, Emma said, 'Hector has been taking the most absurd steps to stop you calling him that name and to win your approval. If you, Mrs Hawkins, want to obtain a job in publishing, and what's more keep the job –'

'Hector Bartlett,' I said, 'is a *pisseur de copie*.' It did me good to repeat the phrase; I enjoyed it. Emma looked at me with a smile that suggested she understood just that.

A taxi drew up full of people. Before Emma went to claim it I said, 'Why don't you give him money to keep away?'

'He'd use it to follow me to America. That's always what people do when you give them money to keep away. They use it contrary to your wishes,' said Emma Loy.

It was well after seven o'clock. Park Lane was full of traffic and people. It had started to rain but there were long bus-queues and I decided it was better to walk and get wet than stand waiting for a bus with its steamy and stuffy interior. What I wondered most on my way home along Park Lane, Knightsbridge, Brompton Road, was how I had never seen Hector Bartlett in the house, at the door, on the stairs, on the landing, and if it was true that he spent a lot of time with Wanda. I was sure Emma had exaggerated; he probably knew poor Wanda casually, and all her cryptic talk and her warnings were simply geared to a wild idea of making Hector's life easier so that she could rid herself of him and his demands, and his knowing her books by heart, and the embarrassments which surely arose when he constituted himself her literary spokesman, as he was already inclined to do.

It was not till over twenty years later that the *Pisseur* started writing his malicious pieces about Emma, and thirty years later that he published his memoirs in which Emma featured in what would have been a sensational light, had his book been capable of attracting any great attention. His fictions about his life with Emma were by then well known; and at that later date she ignored it as she had ignored the *Pisseur*, to his rage all those years, starting about or perhaps before the time when she sat with me at Grosvenor House, trying to get rid of him. Certainly, it seems to me that she already had a fear, a premonition, of the dangers of knowing him.

Splashing home, all wet, in the rain, I thought possibly Hector Bartlett had only seen Wanda once, to get an alteration done. But also, I reflected, it was quite likely that he had come to the house several times. I would ask Milly when she returned, if she remembered anyone of that description coming to the door.

In fact, I have often observed throughout my life that we tend to notice what we expect to notice. I had hardly put myself out to notice Wanda's clients, and I had mostly been away from the house, myself, for long hours every week-day. I was troubled by the thought of Wanda's present condition; I foresaw fuss and nuisance and when I opened my bag to get out my key to the front door, I saw the slip of paper with

Father Stanislas's telephone number. I regretted not telephoning to him. I was very dripping wet.

I knew as I entered the house that there was something wrong. As I mounted the stairs I saw that Wanda's door was open. Voices came from inside. Not the voices of fuss and nuisance, but those of something serious. Wanda must be ill.

William came out followed by Kate, as I reached the first landing.

'What's wrong?' I said.

'Can you come in a minute?' William said. I think the Carlins were there, too, in Wanda's room. A man in a loose trench coat stood there and a young woman who looked official, although she wore no uniform, only a plain brown coat and skirt. No Wanda.

I said, 'Has something happened?'

'Yes,' said the man in the trench coat. 'I'm afraid so.'

'These are the police,' said William. 'Wanda's been drowned.'

It was nearly eight o'clock.

At about seven o'clock, explained the man, police inspector as he was, Mrs Podolak had jumped into the Regent's Canal, and had been fished out too late.

'Nothing you can do to stop these cases,' said the policeman. 'If they want to do it they'll do it.' They had found Wanda's handbag, and got her address from the papers inside it. They had come to see if she had left a letter and find out where her next of kin resided. And he asked me if Wanda had shown any symptoms, anything strange? Had she mentioned suicide?

I told him Wanda had been very strange indeed, for some time. She hadn't mentioned suicide. The others had obviously already given some such information about Wanda. 'And the anonymous letters?' said the policeman. 'Any idea who sent them?'

'No idea. It was a man,' I said, 'because he phoned one night and she heard his voice.' I couldn't believe what had happened, and said so.

'These cases . . .' said the policeman. His female colleague said, 'It's always a shock to everybody.'

'She was a Catholic. I wanted her to see a priest but she didn't want to. A devout Catholic, it's so unlike her to commit suicide. I was going to ring up a Polish priest, anyway, to ask him to come and see her.'

'Catholic doesn't help with an unsound mind,' the policeman said. He spoke with an Irish accent, and probably knew what he was talking about.

I thought of the slip of paper in my bag. I might have been in time.

'You can see by the mess in this room she was of unsound mind,' said Kate. 'The poor woman.'

'Dressmakers are always untidy,' said Eva Carlin. 'Thank God she didn't do it in the house. The poor soul!'

Basil Carlin said, 'The anonymous letters stopped, I seem to think, after she settled up with the income tax. I reckon the letters can't have been the motive. Poor thing!'

'Can any of you suggest a motive?' said the Inspector.

'The motives of suicides', said William, 'are often quite trivial if they exist at all. There was one known to us in the medical school where there had been a row with the laundry, they had lost a pair of this fellow's underdrawers, and he gassed himself.'

The policeman agreed: 'The motives for any crime can be quite futile,' he said.

We were all struck by the word 'crime'; we had been shocked into thinking in terms of Wanda's tragedy.

I wondered wildly if she could have been pushed in. 'Are you sure it was suicide?' I said.

'Witnesses saw her jump. She gave a sort of howl, threw away her handbag and jumped. Someone fished her out but it was too late.'

I told them all that I knew about Wanda's family. Three sisters in Poland, one married in Scotland. No, I didn't know the address in Scotland. Perhaps some cousins in London . . .

The other tenants were murmuring with awe and puffing in distressed exclamation marks after their sad comments. I felt as if we were trespassing in Wanda's room with the two strangers. My clothes felt very wet.

The police sent other men later that night to search Wanda's room. They found her sister's address but no sign of the anonymous letters. Verdict: suicide while of unsound mind.

12

I remembered the wild scream Wanda had given the night before when I had put it to her that I would ring Father Stanislas. I remembered now in greater detail the confusing scene in Wanda's room after we had met at the Carlins to discuss Isobel. Much of it, at the time, had merged into a general impression that she was thoroughly unhinged. 'She needs therapy,' William had said. 'She needs a specialist.' And Wanda's anxiety, when I was talking on the phone to Emma Loy that morning, lest I was ringing Father Stanislas on her behalf; that wail of hers again, as she ran upstairs: it was the last I had heard or seen of Wanda. She was afraid, plainly, of mild Father Stanislas, or something he stood for; she was afraid of something being revealed.

'The motives for suicides are often quite trivial,' William had said. Trivial to the rest of us, but not to them, obviously not to them. I realized how very little I knew about Wanda, far less her mind. It was strange that Emma Loy had been discussing her with me, probably at the very moment when she gave her last cry and jumped into the dark, cold canal. 'The motives quite trivial . . .' Yes, but not to Wanda, not to Wanda.

I remember hardly anything about what I did or said after the police left, that night of Wanda's death.

Somebody in the house rang Milly's daughter in Cork to warn her of the event. Milly herself rang back, and asked for me.

'Why don't you stay there, Milly, till it all blows over?'

Milly wouldn't hear of this. And she wasted no sympathy on Wanda. 'The nerve of the woman,' said Milly, 'to commit suicide from my house!'

For some odd reason this made me feel better. Milly's point of view always offered an element of defiant courage. I looked forward to Milly's return.

After the inquest and the funeral Wanda's sister from Scotland came to the house to collect Wanda's possessions. The others were all out at work. I let her into Wanda's room and asked if I could help her. She said no, she could manage by herself, but I could see she was in a daze, vaguely lifting things up and putting them down in the same place. She was a darker version of Wanda. Her name was Greta; she spoke in a slightly broken English with a Scottish accent.

Now, I had to remind her that all the stuff piled about the room was not necessarily Wanda's. Some, I said, belonged to her clients, and generally speaking we would be safe in assuming that only the clothes which were packed in Wanda's suitcases, or folded in the drawers, or hanging in the wardrobe, were Wanda's property. And even then, I said, sometimes Wanda used to hang up in her wardrobe special dresses she had made for her ladies: one would have to judge by size. For the rest we would have to wait, I rattled on, until the clients came to collect their clothes.

'They're not all women's clothes,' said Greta, fingering through a pile.

'No,' I said, 'Wanda was very clever at altering men's clothes. The owners will turn up for them.'

'Those photographs on the mantelpiece,' said Greta. She sat down and started to cry. 'The bed's not even made,' she said, and picked up a pair of Wanda's well-worn shoes.

'The photographs are undoubtedly Wanda's,' I said. 'Look for an empty suitcase and start putting the photographs together. I'm going to get some newspaper to wrap them in and bring you a cup of tea.'

The sadness of these last gatherings of personal effects, the siftings and sortings and parcelling-up, is more inexpressible than the funeral, where at least there is a fixed rite, there are words, the coffin has a shape and the grave a certain depth, and even the sorrow of the mourners has some silent eloquence if only conveyed and formally interpreted by their standing still. But the grief which is latent in relics like Wanda's pair of worn shoes has no equivalent at all.

When I returned with the tea Greta was examining her sister's bank deposit book. 'Six hundred and thirty pounds,' said Greta. 'I'd no idea she was so well off.' I was called away again just then to answer the doorbell. It was Abigail, Ian Tooley's secretary. She had come primarily to see me, she said, and also to take away some radionics equipment which Wanda had on loan.

I doubted she had come mainly for my sake, but I appreciated Abigail's politeness. I took her up to Wanda's room and, avoiding the big mouthful of Abigail's name, introduced them as Abigail and as Mrs Podolak's sister Greta. Abigail murmured that she was sorry to hear of the tragedy.

'Abigail would like to take away certain equipment that belongs to someone else,' I said. 'In fact I think it's that black box over there. And maybe those books and manuals stacked beside it.'

'Yes,' said Abigail, 'the literature is Mr Tooley's as well.'

'Do you have a receipt for them, Miss?' said Greta, surprisingly awakened out of her vagueness. I was equally surprised to hear Abigail say that she had all the documents with her, and a letter to authorize her to take Mr Tooley's property away. Greta seemed to understand this, and immediately got out her glasses to examine the business on hand, while I stood there marvelling at the acuity of both sides. I had already had some experience of death in my family, and I had been struck, there too, by the way in which people who were stricken with sorrow would be able to deal with rapid lucidity with anything concerning what they conceived to be valuables; and that any claimants to goods in possession of the dead person, or creditors, seemed to have all their documents and receipts ready to present. To see Abigail, efficiently explaining the papers to Greta, and Greta earnestly examining them, one might have thought they had both foreseen and prepared for Wanda's death.

I went to get some tea for Abigail and left them getting down to business.

'But Wanda was a good Catholic!' was what Greta was saying when I returned with fresh tea for Abigail. Greta appealed to me: 'Wanda was devout, no?'

'I believe she was,' I said.

'There is some old Catholics, her friends, told me she shouldn't have had a Catholic burial by reason she committed suicide. But I say she was devout and the Father would not have given her a Catholic funeral if she wasn't all right with the Church.'

'The verdict was unsound mind,' I said. 'It's an illness like any other. She wasn't to blame for it.'

'But now I see she practised this magic,' said Greta. 'This black box of works.'

'It's supposed to do good to people,' said Abigail. 'It isn't magic, as I say, it's radionics. It's supposed to work cures on people thousands of miles away.'

'Take away that box, girl,' said Greta, 'and all the books. I have to tell the priest about it. Yes, it's on my conscience.'

I had in my mind's ears that cry of Wanda's when I had offered to talk to Father Stanislas. That cry, that cry. Wanda, in her madness, had been terrorized. And her fearful suspicion, that morning, when I had spoken on the phone to Emma: 'You spoke to Father Stanislas. I heard you . . .' Her wail, as she ran upstairs. 'Is it my fault you are ill? You are wasting. You will die,' she had said the day before.

I determined to get out of Abigail what Wanda was doing with that radionics instrument, or rather, what she thought she was doing. If it hadn't been that Wanda evidently had it in her disordered mind that she was doing me some harm, I would have taken no further interest. Wanda was dead. People commit suicide for quite trivial reasons, William had said. But whatever Wanda's reasons I was disturbed by the words that had involved me in her mind, 'You are wasting. You will die,' when in fact I had no previous idea that I was specially in her mind at all.

'Don't go just yet,' I said to Abigail.

'No, I'm not going. There's something I came to talk to you about.'

So Abigail stayed and helped us to pack Wanda's boxes, to sort out in separate piles the clothes that were obviously Wanda's and those that were presumably her customers'. In the wardrobe was a man's suit of clothes, an ordinary dark-blue suit. I grabbed it and said, 'This must be a client's.' It flashed through my mind immediately that it might be Hector Bartlett's. I remembered what Emma had told me: 'Hector has been taking the most absurd steps to stop you calling him by that name . . .'

Now, holding this man's suit in my hand, I was convinced that Hector Bartlett had been somehow using Wanda to work against me. Isobel introduced him to Wanda to have his dinner suit altered. 'I think it all began last summer and he met you in the park . . .' – I could hear Emma Loy's words. But already, Wanda had been blackmailed by Hector Bartlett, probably seduced, the foolish woman. And he had gone on to use Wanda, and used her beyond her endurance. Because I had insulted him in the park . . . The theory grew in my mind, wild as it was, and took various forms. I filled in details.

Abigail waited till Greta had left in a taxi with her first load of stuff. Greta was to return next day to go through Wanda's letters and papers, and see what she could throw away. We had already glanced through them, with the police, to see if there was any due to Wanda's death, but it appeared the papers were all old receipts and even older letters written in Polish, mixed up with old photographs.

I have always liked Abigail de Mordell Staines-Knight, as she then was, Abigail Wilson as she is now. It turned out to be true she had come to Church End Villas that day primarily to see me, and only incidentally to claim back the Box. She told me she was leaving Mackintosh & Tooley's to join the staff of an interesting new magazine, the *Highgate Review*, so called because the editors, a group of American refugees from Senator McCarthy's political persecutions, had settled in Highgate. The *Highgate Review* would be devoted to cultural and political events. They needed a capable managing editor. 'So I thought of you, Mrs Hawkins. They don't pay much but it could be a wonderful job. Would you be interested?'

My savings were getting low and I felt ready for a new job. Abigail agreed to arrange for me to go for an interview. I would have shown more enthusiasm then and there, if I had not had heavily weighing on my mind the mystery of Wanda's suicide and my suspicions of Hector Bartlett's involvement in it, which I was to talk to William about later that night. If Wanda's belief that I was wasting away because of some curse she had put on me was sincere, she was totally mistaken. But the fact that anyone should wish me ill to such an extent appalled me, already depressed as I was by Wanda's death.

I sat with Abigail in Milly's kitchen, thinking of the *Pisseur*'s suit, as I thought it was, hanging upstairs in Wanda's wardrobe. I only half-listened to Abigail's deb-chat conversation, which usually I found very diverting. I had known, before Emma Loy told me, that I had made an enemy of

Hector Bartlett on the morning in Green Park when I had hissed in his face '*Pisseur de copie*'. Since then I had lost two jobs for this crime and the repetition of it, and I didn't think of repenting. On the contrary, I had counted it one of the prime duties of the jobs.

'And the name of the party,' Abigail was saying in her description of one of the founders of the *Highgate Review*, 'is Howard Send. Too killing. I called him Passage to India, he was amazed. Of course, he's that way, but they often make better friends.'

I agreed to go for an interview with Howard Send. 'Abigail,' I said, 'tell me about this Box of yours.'

'Not mine, it's Ian Tooley's. He's a spiritualist, you know, and a psychic researcher, all that. I'm really sorry for his wife because he's rather sweet in spite of it all.'

'How did he get hold of Wanda Podolak?'

'She's on his list, introduced by a general organizer who hasn't any skill at it himself, but he's clever at finding people who are, Hector Bartlett, you know, that hanger-on of Emma Loy's. He's the organizer, gosh, isn't he awful? Imagine him running around with a sample of your blood or a strand of your hair and trying to get someone to diagnose what's wrong with you.'

'Surely he doesn't believe in it?' I said.

'Ardently,' said Abigail, 'unutterably ardently.'

'I can't imagine that man being sincere about anything,' I said.

'But his operators get results. Apparently they get amazing results. Ian Tooley gets letters from grateful patients, I've seen the letters.'

'About Hector Bartlett?'

'About him, yes. They say he's a wonder at the Box. They don't know he doesn't do it himself, but of course he does teach his operators, so in a way he deserves the credit. Personally, I can't stand the man, frightfully smarmy.'

'Why doesn't he stick to radionics as a profession, I wonder? Why does he try to write?'

'I suppose he wants to see his name in print, and be famous. You know how they all do. Ian Tooley has tried to reason with him, but he considers himself a great critic, a sort of thinker.'

'He's a *pisseur de copie*,' I said.

Abigail was delighted. 'The French', she said, 'always have a word for it, don't they? You're looking so very young these days, Mrs Hawkins.'

'I'm not so very old,' I said.

Much later that night when I propounded to William, in its various stages of logic, my theory about the *Pisseur*'s influence on Wanda, I was persuaded to discard it. 'First of all,' William said, 'that blue suit in Wanda's wardrobe is mine and I'll thank you to hand it over. It's the only decent suit I've got.'

William said other things that sounded like common sense. I forget what they were. But the fact that I had jumped to the wrong conclusion about the owner of the suit in Wanda's wardrobe waylaid me into doubting my own suspicions about Hector Bartlett's relationship with Wanda. I was anxious to impress William with my reasonability and intelligence. But in fact William was wrong and I had been quite near the truth.

Radionics was already flourishing in England by the mid-'fifties. It was a pseudo-scientific practice that had started in the United States in the early part of the twentieth century. It claimed to diagnose and cure at any distance disorders and ailments in people, animals and vegetables. It gained a following, and today still enjoys a considerable number of believers. That it is a totally irrational method of healing is not to discount it and certainly the claims of 'radionics' (the word is not in the dictionary) are no more a subject for mockery than the claims of all our religions. Personally, I think it a lot of bosh and object to the tenacious efforts of the practitioners over the years to establish a scientific basis for the efficacy of this Box with its coloured liquids, its bit of hair on a metal plate, its rows of knobs which the operators twiddle, its claptrap about ratings, coded instructions, electromagnetic fields, its chabras (rays) and its L-fields (life), T-fields (thought), its O-fields (organizing), and its emanations. Oh God! – the Box has no relation to any scientific instrument; it is not electronic, it is not electrical; it has no radiation. It was discredited in the United States, but not in England where to-day farmers put their crops on the Box and horse-trainers their sick horses.

In 1955 I knew much less about what the Box claims to do than I do now. At the time I had only two clear ideas about it, which I still hold. The first was that it was a crank activity, not necessarily fake in that its practitioners and followers were apparently in good faith. The second was the purely academic proposition that if the Box is able to do good it follows logically that it is capable of doing harm. So that if you believe it can bless the crops then it can curse the weeds. If you believe it can affect your health beneficially, then you have to believe it can affect it malevolently. My advice to anyone who wants to try the Box is, treat it as an experience but believe nothing. And above all, don't spend much of your good money on it.

Before Abigail left I asked if I could borrow some of the literature on the subject, which she had taken from Wanda's room. She lent me a book and a pamphlet. I wanted to see if I could find how Wanda had worked it out that through her efforts I was wasting away. I couldn't make head or tail of the mumbo-jumbo, and in fact spent very little effort in trying to grasp what radionics was all about.

In a later publication I saw the claim that with a sample of hair or blood it was possible to treat someone radionically without their knowledge. The Radionics Association, formed in 1960, 'prohibits this practice'. But since there is no way of enforcing such a rule, these 'prohibitions' are worthless. Some publications, which I have consulted to refresh my opinion of what happened in 1955, confirmed my disbelief in the efficacy of the practice. The subject was aired in the High Court of Justice in a famous case of 1960, when it was generally established that while the Box had no scientific basis for its diagnostic claims, the practitioners and their followers might be perfectly sincere. A large number of medical witnesses said the Box was utter rubbish, and a large number of respectable people said it wasn't. And I daresay that from the point of view of a visitor from outer space the Box is no more ridiculous than a Catholic catechism or the Mass.

When I returned to my real young life, later that night, William made me laugh about my 'wasting away'. I thought he was unduly callous about Wanda's madness, but at the same time I saw he was trying to lift my spirits out of morbid reflections, and he succeeded. He had a fine collection of gramophone records.

I went by tube on the Northern line to Highgate for my interview next morning. I had had enough of the buses of my long, sad peregrinations during the past month.

Abigail was waiting to introduce me.

'How do you do, Mr Send.'

'Nice to see you, Mrs Hawkins.'

Abigail went to another room to wait for me and file her nails. I got the job, on the basis of a month's trial starting early April, which was the next week. 'When you are editing copy, Mrs Hawkins, what sort of things do you look for?' said Howard Send. 'Exclamation marks and italics used for emphasis,' I said. 'And I take them out.' It was as good an answer as any. 'Suppose the author was Aldous Huxley or Somerset Maugham?' he said. I told him that if these were his authors he didn't need a copy-editor. 'Too true,' he said. He pointed to some piles of manuscripts on another desk. 'We have to look through all those. But they aren't by Maugham or Huxley.'

The place they had rented in Highgate was a tall Victorian house, not unlike Milly's in South Kensington, only wider. My job there was the most interesting and amusing one of my life. The excitement was purely connected with events and people. But when, in my waking hours of the night, I look back at 'Highgate' as an experience I think of it as shell-pink. This can be partly explained. First, it was Howard Send's habit to bring in armfuls of flowers to the house, tall pale apple, pear, peach and plum-blossom, white and pink, forming an all-over pink effect. Tulips and bowls of hyacinths too, but it is one of my memory's impressions, rather than a memory, that I am describing. I think Howard's friend and editorial partner, Fred Tucher (pronounced Toocher) wore one of the first men's pink shirts I had seen. One way and the other, I see it in shell-pink. The sitting-room was a large front room across the hall from an equally proportioned room which formed the office. Both had bow windows. The sitting-room had very deep and comfortable beige-covered sofas and chairs; the office had a light wall-to-wall carpet, pale walls, light wooden desks and shelves.

And shell-pink is what emerges as a general effect. Perhaps, if I delved deeper into this impression it would emerge that my memory is coloured shell-pink by the tepid politics of the refugee Highgate set. I had expected them to be rabid reds or extremists of the left as their enemies in America claimed, and I had always associated people of crusader-like left-wing leanings with grim faces and glum rectitude, with plans and statistics, and coming home from night schools at the London School of Economics, in the rain, sucking acid drops. But the Highgate set were moneyed and sophisticated. Their politics were more or less liberal. They were so like the ordinary educated English in their tastes and ideas that one wondered how they could possibly have been accused, as they had been, of allegiances with the rigid Soviets. In fact they were simply typical expatriate Americans, with an abundance of money at the current rate of exchange, culturally informed, and very much at home in England. I had not travelled much at that time, or I would have known that many other Americans were becoming very much at home, too, in France and Italy.

On that day of my interview Howard Send said, 'Well, thanks, Mrs Hawkins, you're hired for a month's trial. We're on first-name terms around here. I'm Howard. You're Agnes, I take it?' I said, 'Nancy.'

'Well, Nancy, see you next week. You'll find plenty to do.'

Abigail and I found somewhere to lunch. We decided we could largely make what we liked of the job, and went on to talk of more important things, such as Abigail's passion for Giles Wilson who had a job in Lloyd's to which he went bowler-hatted every week-day morning, and whose evenings were devoted to managing and supporting a small pioneer rock-and-roll group. He fitted Abigail into these evenings, which she loved, and took her away for weekends in the country to as many of their friends as would have them, preference being given to those who didn't have big dinner parties on Saturday nights, 'and make you help with the washing-up on Sunday.' Abigail's parents were divorced. Her father, she told me, lived with some sisters and male cousins in a big old house 'where you have to make yourself useful the minute you put your foot in the door. You spend all your weekend outside getting the tomatoes or vegetables or eggs or picking strawberries, and inside, cleaning the silver which they save up for you to do. All that, so that everyone can sit round the table sticking their fork into a brussel-sprout and expressing adulation for Anthony Eden.' Nor did Abigail care to spend weekends at Giles's family home which was a charming converted barn, but with too small a family for her to sleep with Giles: 'In a house like that you would be noticed.' They intended to get married as soon as they had the money for the honeymoon, which might be next year.

I loved Abigail's knack of portraying her world in these inconsequential phrases, without any rancour, explanations or many details.

I told her I was looking for a small flat.

'I like your digs in Kensington,' she said.

So I told her about William, and how we intended to set up together and get married when he had passed his finals. She said she would keep a look-out for a cheap flat. We went home together as far as Knightsbridge where Abigail left me with a flick of her red scarf. I was feeling restored, for the moment thinking of my new job and William, instead of that death, that death, of Wanda.

It was just after three when I got home, to find Milly's suitcases in the hallway. She had just arrived back from Ireland, almost at the same time as Wanda's sister had turned up to go through the last remains of Wanda's property. I found Milly upstairs in Wanda's room with Greta.

'Milly, oh, Milly,' I said, standing in the door.

'How thin you are, Mrs Hawkins. Are you all right?' Milly said.

'Do call me Nancy,' I said.

'Are you well?'

In fact I had been getting thinner before Milly had left, but so gradually, she hadn't noticed. I told her I was feeling fine. Nothing, however, then or later, would remove from Milly's mind the idea that the shock of Wanda's death had affected me in such a rapid and dramatic way as to reduce my former bulk by half.

'You see what happens,' she said to Greta who was sitting

by the window looking through a bundle of photographs – 'You see what happens when this sort of thing happens? It happens that people's hair goes white overnight and they waste away. Suicide, and a person in my house.'

Greta hardly noticed Milly's agitation; it seemed she was puzzling over the photographs.

I went into the room and tried to calm Milly down.

'Most of her things, her clothes, went yesterday,' I said. 'Let's go through the rest and finish. Would you like a cup of tea?'

'Later,' said Milly. 'There are things to do here.' I had never seen her so agitated. She had taken out a drawer full of old-looking papers, letters, bills of no account dating from five years back. Obviously Wanda had been a hoarder. 'What I'm looking for,' said Milly, 'is one of those anonymous letters. Someone drove Wanda to suicide.'

'They certainly did,' said Greta.

The drawer full of papers was on Wanda's bed. Milly and I sat, one on each side of it, Milly fingering the papers aimlessly. Greta put aside her bundle of photographs and took up another bundle from the dressing-table. Watching them for a moment it struck me they were trying to reconstruct Wanda, and I thought of a passage in *Frankenstein* where the scientist-narrator dabbles in the grave for materials to construct his monster. I have looked up this passage. Here it is precisely:

Who shall conceive the horrors of my secret toil, as I dabbled among the unhallowed damps of the grave, or tortured the living animal to animate the lifeless clay?

That is putting it strongly in the literal sense, but it portrays the impression I had, there in Wanda's room, while we looked through Wanda's pitiful papers.

I started putting the contents of the drawer in a preliminary order – letters here, postcards there, old bills elsewhere. With my office training I was able to do this quickly. There were five or six little piles. Then I started putting each pile in date order. 'Most of this stuff is useless,' I said.

'Any sign of those anonymous letters?' said Milly. 'Look carefully.'

'No, Wanda must have destroyed them.'

I felt it necessary to say something about Wanda's merits.

'She was a very good dressmaker,' I said, inspired by an old receipt for threequarters of a yard of *moiré* ribbon, 'and very reasonable in her prices.'

'A hard-working woman,' said Milly.

'She didn't deserve it,' said Greta.

I could tell that Milly really wanted to agree to this proposition, but that her Catholic beliefs wouldn't let her go so far as to attribute the victim's role to Wanda. She tried to speak, but didn't.

Greta said, looking at me for confirmation, 'They gave her a Catholic burial. Unsound mind is a disease like any other.'

Milly brightened at this news. 'Is that a fact?' she said.

'Somebody or something turned her brain,' I said.

'That I believe,' said Milly.

'What a fool,' said Greta.

'It looks as if she owes nothing. There are no bills unpaid,' I said.

'Her rent,' said Greta. 'She didn't pay her last week's rent, did she? – I'll pay it.'

'Nothing of the kind,' said Milly. 'I wouldn't touch her last week's rent. It would be blood money.'

Among the correspondence, I was looking only for the handwriting as I remembered it of the first anonymous letter, but I found nothing resembling it. Most of the letters were from Poland, and written in Polish; evidently the postcards were those sent from friends on holiday. There was one from Kate, one from myself. I handed the bundle to Greta. 'You'd better take these home and destroy what you don't want to keep,' I said.

'And the photographs?' said Greta, as if asking for permission.

'They're all yours,' I said. 'We can destroy these old bills and things.'

'The photographs I don't know how to explain,' Greta said. 'There are snaps of the family, our sisters in Poland, and me, and our children. There is the uncle and our two aunties. That is good. But here is some photos, I don't know what.' She handed me a postcard-sized photograph. 'It's Wanda's face, but that isn't Wanda. And who is the fellow?'

I saw immediately that the fellow was Hector Bartlett, *pisseur de copie*. He was standing beside a girl, or at least it was Wanda's face poised on a girl's shape, not Wanda's. It was a model girl's shape dressed in a neat shirt and slinky trousers. The background was a sea-front, somewhere like Margate or Ramsgate. Obviously the photograph was faked. However, it was harmless. I showed it to Milly, and not to alarm her with what was really beginning to go on in my mind, I said, 'This has been faked, it's a joke, Wanda's head on another woman's body. Do you recognize that man with her?'

Milly said at once, 'That's one of her cousins.'

'What cousin?' said Greta.

'The cousin that's studying for the priesthood, a late vocation,' Milly said.

'We have no such cousin,' said Greta. 'I never saw that person before.'

Milly was aghast. I thought she was inclined to disbelieve Greta.

'Did he come to see her?' I said.

'Often,' said Milly. 'He came often in the afternoon to keep Wanda company, after all that shock she had with the letters.'

'He is no cousin,' Greta said.

I said, 'I never saw him here.'

'Oh, you were out at work. He had to get back to his seminary at five, don't forget. There's surely no harm in him,' said Milly.

'There is no such cousin,' Greta said.

'She told me he was her cousin, a student priest.' Milly was agitated.

'It was a joke,' I said. 'Like the photo. A harmless joke.'

'Some joke!' said Greta. 'Look at these other pictures.'

The other pictures were equally harmless, Wanda and Hector in the street, Wanda in her normal dumpy guise but Hector with his face imposed upon another, a small man's body. There was a picnic photograph, both Wanda and Hector Bartlett faked into an elegant pose they couldn't possibly have assumed in real life. I took the photographs from Greta and went through them. I found five of these obvious fakes. Then

I found one without Wanda. It showed Hector Bartlett and a short man standing in profile. They were feeding ducks on a lake which I couldn't identify. I thought I vaguely recognized the man in profile but couldn't place him at the time.

I turned all the photographs over to see if there was anything written on the back and, finding nothing, returned them to Greta. 'Take them away,' I said.

'It's a mystery,' said Greta.

'Fancy him fooling me,' said Milly. 'I thought he was a seminarian.'

I bustled to get a suitcase from the top of the wardrobe in order to pack Wanda's final things. I wanted to get rid of Greta but I knew my thoughts would take shape later on, perhaps in the course of my waking night. We made a separate package of Wanda's correspondence; we packed the suitcase with the belongings of Wanda's clients which Greta was arranging to leave with a friend in London whose address she gave to Milly. We put the old bills in a heap to throw away. There were various untidy and useless odds and ends and scraps of old paper left in some of the drawers. 'Leave them to me,' said Milly. 'I'll clear them all up tomorrow.'

She took Greta downstairs for a cup of tea. We called a taxi, and sent her away. Milly was tired after her journey, and anguished by the disaster that had come into her life. 'I wonder why that fellow said he was her cousin? A student priest . . .'

'Forget it for now, Milly,' I said. 'You'll feel better in the morning. And so will I.' I was upset that the latest perplexities of Wanda's death had put out of my mind, for the rest of the afternoon, the prospective happiness of my new job, and the beautiful story, as it seemed to me, of Abigail and Giles, he with his bowler hat going to work at Lloyd's and in the evening going to manage his rock-and-roll group. I wanted a flat to share with William. In fact I was good and tired of being Mrs Hawkins. I wanted to be Nancy with my new good shape.

The telephone rang shortly after Greta's taxi had driven away. We had wished her a good journey home. We had told her not to worry. I was going to sit Milly down and give her a drink.

I answered the phone. 'Mrs Hawkins, I wonder if you would be free for dinner one evening this week, perhaps Friday or Saturday? I want your advice about Isobel. She's having difficulty settling in to the new flat. Curtains and so forth. And besides, we could have a rollicking good time, you and I, if you . . .'

'No, Mr Lederer, it's not possible.'

Your advice, Mrs Hawkins . . . Was I still Mrs Hawkins with my face superimposed on the shape of another woman, like Wanda's in the photograph?

Later that evening we had a sort of wake for Wanda; the tenants collected in the kitchen round Milly to welcome her home and keep her company in the astonishing course of events; in her absence, Isobel had left the house, pregnant, and Wanda had jumped in the canal. Some show of solidarity was called for.

The news about Isobel did not shake Milly very much, especially as she had already left the house.

'She was too much indulged by her father. What can you expect?' said Milly. 'But I wouldn't have expected it of Wanda

Podolak,' she said more than once, as if suicide and having a baby outside of marriage were equals in disaster. But, deeply, I knew that she was far more disturbed by Wanda's death than she could express. 'I wouldn't have believed it of Wanda . . .' sounded in my ear like that legendary rebuke of the Edinburgh landlady to James Simpson, the nineteenth-century pioneer of chloroform, who, experimenting on himself, was found unconscious on the floor of his room, and was presumed drunk: 'I wouldn't have thought it of you, Mr Simpson.'

Working people as we were, nobody remembered seeing Hector Bartlett whose visits as Wanda's cousin had been timed, I supposed, to avoid us. 'I thought he was a young gentleman. I never would have suspected that of Wanda,' said Milly. And I realized she now assumed he had been Wanda's lover. Perhaps he had. For my part, I kept quiet about him. Not a word about his name or identity or the fact I had recognized him in the photographs. I was sitting there with William beside me, Kate, the Carlins. Mr Twinny the odd-job man and his wife looked in, also, to greet Milly and make awesome remarks about Wanda's fate. It was strange how everyone remembered what they were doing when they heard the news of Wanda's death and described the moment to Milly. Kate had opened the door to the police: 'Is this where a Mrs W. Podolak lives . . .?' And Kate described her feelings as she took them upstairs, knocking on the door of the Carlins' room. The Carlins recalled their frozen horror, and Basil Carlin had called William to his wife's white-faced aid. Mr Twinny got the news from someone in the street, 'and I went home and I told Mrs Twinny to sit down and take it easy, and I broke the news.' William said he was of course horrified, 'but you get used to situations where people are brought in to the hospital after accidents, you don't have to take it too personally.' All these testimonies helped Milly. I wasn't able to contribute greatly. My mind wasn't so much on what I was doing when I heard the news. 'I came home wet through,' I said, 'to find the police up in Wanda's room.' But I was really thinking of what I was doing at the time she took the plunge: in Grosvenor House with Emma Loy, discussing Hector Bartlett, with the telephone number of Father Stanislas in my handbag.

In the course of the reunion I was called again to the telephone. It was Isobel Lederer. She wanted me to do something for her, and I completely forget what. But I can still hear two bright and confident phrases: 'I know I can depend on you, Mrs Hawkins' (Oh, can you? I thought), and 'You won't let me down, I know, Mrs Hawkins' (Oh, won't I?). Whatever the errand or the favour she wanted, whether I promised to do it or not, I didn't do it.

Lying awake in the night I saw again those grotesque photographs of Hector Bartlett and Wanda. It came to me quite easily who the short man was who had appeared with Hector in profile: the blighted Vladimir, who used to flit round the offices of Mackintosh & Tooley. Fake White Russian as he was, with his embittered camera, it was well within his scope to confection these fake-photographs of Wanda. I wondered why she had kept them, and considered it probable that there had been others, possibly of Wanda's face mounted on a pornographically posed body, that she had fearfully destroyed or had been shown by way of blackmail. This was a supposition that I was never able to verify. In piecing together the jig-saw pieces of Hector Bartlett's involvement in Wanda's suicide I wasn't able to explain with certainty the scope of those pathetic fake photographs and I am left with the memory of Greta's bewilderment and Milly's puzzled horror, that day on my return from Highgate when we looked at the bundles of photographs in Wanda's room. I began to think of Wanda in a new light. Emma Loy's story, combined with my own new love affair with William, had opened my eyes. I have noticed that people in love and having a love affair are more aware of the sexual potential in others than those who are not. In the years since my first husband's death, when I hadn't been in love, it hadn't occurred to me that some of the people I knew might be amorously involved, unless they actually told me so or had got engaged. What did I really know of all the people I had met in the offices where I had worked, day after day? What did I know of Kate? Or of Isobel, perhaps in love with someone, not the father of her child? What had I ever known of Wanda?

I thought of that day when, after one of her long, terrible cries, Milly and I had run up to Wanda's room and found her in bed; I had fleetingly noticed, had not perhaps noticed enough, how attractive, bedworthy, she looked with her fair hair down around her shoulders. Not having a lover myself at the time, I saw and didn't see. I had thought of Wanda as the plump Polish dressmaker, her life full of church and friends and enemies, of Madonnas and novenas and her ladies who came for fittings. The last thing I would have thought was that she might have a lover.

I thought of it now, and I thought of Hector Bartlett then as a psychological case and a dangerous one. A lonely middle-aged widow, and Hector Bartlett banally insinuating himself into her life and feelings, mesmerizing and blackmailing the silly woman with a view to forcing her to work that absurd Box. Was that melodrama possible? I decided that it was. Ageing women were seduced by ruthless men every day. Since then I have seen it happen to women of high intellectual qualities. I have known a woman doctor on holiday in Italy who was seduced and pickpocketed by a man calling himself an airline official at the Trevi fountain; it wouldn't have mattered, but she took it to heart. I knew of a woman governor of a prison who fell in love with one of the inmates, who was serving time for murdering his wife; it wouldn't have mattered, but she lost her job. What chance, what protection against herself, had Wanda?

Next morning, just when I was thinking that my notions formed in the quiet night might be rather too wild, Milly came up to my room.

'I've been clearing up Wanda's room, and I found this stuff under the mattress,' said Milly.

There were two press-cuttings, one tiny, one longer, and three small crumpled envelopes. I looked first at the envelopes because on one of them was written 'Haukens' which I took to be Wanda's spelling of my name. On the other two envelopes were written respectively 'Stoke' and 'Asherbi'. Who these last two names referred to I was never to find out. Inside each envelope was a small cutting of hair neatly bound with a piece of thread. The hair of 'Haukens' seemed exactly my own, but at the moment I couldn't think how Wanda could have obtained it.

'She used hairs to work a silly box for curing people,' I said to Milly.

'It makes me feel awful,' Milly said. She sat down, handing me the press-cuttings. 'Read these,' said Milly.

By my editorial training I looked first, automatically, to see what newspaper the cuttings came from. There was no indication. No name or date was either printed or written on the cuttings. On the back of each cutting was a roughly printed news item, both disjointed and unintelligible scraps such as appear on the backs of all press-cuttings. But it wasn't an expert job.

The small piece was from a presumptive Personal column. It read: 'South Kensington Dressmaker specializing alterations Wanda Podolak phone for fittings all hours.' This was followed by our phone number.

The longer piece, apparently a news item, was headed 'Polish Dressmaker Under Investigation'. It began:

Police are investigating the activities of a Polish lady resident in our country with headquarters in Kensington who advertises regularly in the Personal columns of our newspapers. Invariably, the Personal message comes in the following apparently innocent words. [The Personal advertisement in the small press-cutting repeated.]

But what is behind this message? The lady in question, Mrs Wanda Podolak, of 14 Church End Villas, South Kensington explained in an interview, 'I am only trying to help people. There is nothing malign whatsoever in my activities. It is not true that I practise witchcraft or try to alter the personality of my clients by means of radionics. It is not true that I obtain snippings of their hair when they come to have their clothes fitted. I am a bona fide dressmaker and a practising Catholic.'

The police deny they are investigating the case of a young woman who has begun to lose weight mysteriously after being treated by radionics at the establishment of Mrs Podolak in the respectable Victorian house in Church End Villas where the 'dressmaker' operates. 'If the young lady in question has complained that she is wasting away,' said the police spokesman, 'we are not aware of it and if we were we would advise her to see a doctor.' The spokesman admitted, however, that they were looking into other aspects of a possible 'racket' being conducted at 14 Church End Villas.

'The cheek of it,' said Milly. 'In the papers. What do you make of it?'

I said, 'These are not real press cuttings. They are fake. Honestly, Milly, they never appeared in any newspaper. That man who posed as Wanda's cousin had them made up to play a trick on her. I happen to know where he had them specially printed. A Mr Wells at Notting Hill, a perfectly nice printing shop. I'll take you there, and I'm sure he'll confirm it.'

I did take Milly and the press-cuttings to Mr Wells, and he did confirm that they were part of Hector Bartlett's special orders. But even if I hadn't already known about Hector Bartlett's confections of press-cuttings, certainly I wouldn't have been taken in by these scraps of paper. Mr Wells was not such a fine artist as to reproduce a newspaper cutting which would appear authentic to anyone used to handling them. Mr Wells was concerned that his work had upset Milly. Cathy was hanging about outside his office as we talked.

'Are there any copies of these?' I said.

'No, I only made one copy each. Very expensive, but he paid. Might I ask what use he made of them?'

'Only a joke,' I said. 'Let's tear them up.' And we tore them up then and there.

'A very bad joke,' said Milly. 'Mentioning my house.'

We went to tea with Cathy, and Milly cheered up as she always did when she met some new human being. Cathy committed herself so far as to say that Hector Bartlett with his tricks was dangerous, and Mr Wells was a fool, though he meant no harm.

'Do you think,' said Milly, 'that the sight of those words in the press sent Wanda to her death?'

I was inclined to think so. But how could I explain this malignity to Milly? I believed that Hector Bartlett had put every sort of pressure on Wanda. He had used terror, sex, the persuasions of love, the threats of exposure to induce her to work the Box against who knew what people before me? My crime had been to call him to his face *pisseur de copie*. I intended to do so again.

'Quite futile motives . . .' William had said about suicide in general. 'Often, something quite trivial . . .' I suppose if we had taken our story and the press-cuttings and the bits of hair to the police they might have done some token thing, like questioning Hector Bartlett. But he need only have explained that it was a joke. In any case I wasn't about to involve Milly and her 14 Church End Villas in any more of this upset. Wanda was dead. And, certainly, of unsound mind. I felt bad about not getting the priest to her in time.

It was after six when on the way home in the bus I remembered how Wanda had altered a round-necked dress, to make it more fashionably lower. Snip, snip, went her scissors round my neck, cutting V-shapes in that expert way that dressmakers have. That must have been how she got my piece of hair.

Realizing this, I felt suddenly claustrophobic. I said to Milly, 'I've found a job, starting next week. That gives us three clear days. Let's go to Paris tomorrow.'

Milly had never been 'abroad'. But just as if I had said, 'Let's go to the pictures tomorrow,' she turned her blue eyes on me. 'OK,' she said.

13

It is a good thing to go to Paris for a few days if you have had a lot of trouble, and that is my advice to everyone except Parisians.

Milly, who was at home everywhere, made herself at home in Paris to the extent that immediately on our arrival at the hotel she found herself indispensably involved in coping with a girl who, at that very moment, had a miscarriage in the entrance hall. Somehow, although she knew no French, Milly sent porters, bellboys, maids and myself flying to right and left for blankets, towels, water, mops and buckets, the doctor and a glass of brandy. Milly took off her coat. She rolled back the cuffs of her blouse. She arranged two chairs for a couch and ordered the girl to be laid upon it. She cleared the hall of unnecessary people. The doctor arrived, the ambulance came. It was all over in about twenty minutes. Milly turned down her cuffs and signed the hotel register.

I think of that three-day trip in terms of Milly's Paris, for it was quite unlike any other visit to Paris I have known; it was full of the Arc de Triomphe, the gilded Joan of Arc, the Eiffel Tower, the Tuileries, and the Mona Lisa. Now, Milly remarked that the Mona Lisa was 'the image of Mrs Twinny,' by which observation I was first amazed and then impressed for, indeed, Mrs Twinny the wife of our odd-job neighbour bore a decided resemblance to the Mona Lisa; I wondered that I had never thought of it and decided that the intellectual practice of associating ideas overlays and obliterates our spontaneous gifts of recognition. Since then I have formed a more observant habit and sometimes I see people I know or have met in the features of a portrait which has nothing else whatsoever to do with the people of my acquaintance. The face of one of Picasso's acrobats looks strikingly like Milly's in her sixties. Many a drawing of Matisse resembles Abigail. One of the Magi in Mostaert's 'Adoration' haunted my memory for days until it came to mind he was the image of that man in a rain-coat who was employed by a creditor of Ullswater Press to stand outside and stare up at the office window in the hope of embarrassing the firm into paying. Cathy is reflected in a family portrait by Degas. The face of the self-portrait of Dürer in the Prado Museum, bearded though it is, resembles both in features and expression that director of Mackintosh & Tooley whose family tragedy clouded her life. And the face of that good woman, Rembrandt's wife dressed up as 'Flora' in the National Gallery of London, bears an intense similarity to Hector Bartlett, *pisseur de copie*, as he appeared in the 1950s. I have seen on a dining-room wall the portrait of a calm, proud and noble ancestor who could have been a male twin of sad Mabel, the distraught wife of Patrick the packer. My advice to anyone who wishes to categorize people by their faces is that physiognomy is a very uncertain guide to their character, intelligence or place in time and society.

Milly bought a blue flowered toque in Paris, into the high crown of which she stuffed some bottles of scent, successfully to wear on her return through the customs.

William was to take his final exams within a few months and had good hopes of getting a job for a year in a big general hospital in London. We decided to find a flat but not to get married till he had actually got his degree and the job. But we had very little time for serious flat-hunting. My new job at Highgate involved long hours of travelling, and the even longer hours of work that are somehow demanded by those easier and more intimate employers than in large formal establishments where the staff comes and goes at fixed hours.

It was true that Abigail and I, as we had decided, could make what we liked of the job. We both did a bit of everything, I mainly doing editorial work and Abigail, secretarial. I read manuscripts and passed them to Howard Send or Fred Tucher with recommendations about acceptance or rejection. If they were accepted I went through them again to make suggestions of all sorts, ranging from punctuation and style to a complete reconstruction. The *Highgate Review* was well enough known, and is still quoted, but for readers before whose time it flourished and who haven't heard of it, here are some of the topics that I recall from among its contributions over the months: the hydrogen bomb and the World Scientists' Appeal for peace, the question of atomic stations and the suspension of nuclear test explosions, a report on an Afro-Asian conference, universal copyright law, the need for smokeless zones in major cities, Germany's joining NATO, the reopening of the Vienna State Opera house, the case for Anglo-Catholicism as against Roman Catholicism, extra-sensory perception. Then there was a literary section with essays on Pablo Neruda, Jean-Paul Sartre, Thomas Mann, Ernest Hemingway. There was an art and music section. Each issue made space for two or three poems.

Howard and Fred were occupied most of the day discussing the articles, forming policy, and talking, among their flowers in the large sitting-room, to the frequent visitors, mainly the authors of the essays. Abigail's jobs, besides composing and typing letters which she was well able to do, included packing suitcases for Howard and Fred when they went away for the weekend, checking their laundry and making coffee. My job, apart from editing, was making omelettes and salads on days when there was little time for lunch.

Abigail and I used often to discuss 'the Boys' as we called them, between ourselves. She said that for her part she found it easier to work for homosexuals than for straight men. 'No personal complications,' she said.

We were impressed by the way the Boys generally got up when we came into the room, unless they were really over-whelmed by work or telephone calls. 'Is that American or is it homosexual?' Abigail wondered. Anyway, I said, I felt we should tell them there was no need.

'No, don't do that,' said Abigail. 'I love it. So refreshing after the manners where I was dragged up.' I was presently to spend a weekend at Sanky Place, the stately pile where Abigail was dragged up. It was true that, to a man, the men grunted when you came into the room, and went on reading the paper, sometimes shifting their behinds with a slight shuffling movement of acknowledgement. According to Abigail, when she went in to announce the fact that she was going to marry Giles Wilson, they just went on grunting.

Abigail came to work in a small Austin car she had acquired. But I had to leave Church End Villas at a quarter to eight every morning and seldom got home before eight-thirty. None the less, my life was changing for the better, and better still, in the third week after I joined the *Highgate Review*, Howard Send asked me to put an advertisement in the papers, a basement flat to let.

'Do you mean', I said, 'that you have the basement free, here in this house?'

There was a basement flat free, and within our means. 'I'm looking for a flat for my boyfriend William and me,' I said.

I phoned William and he came to look at the flat that evening. It was not too dark, the windows being partly above street level. There was one other occupant, Mrs Thomas, who did the cleaning and shopping for the house. 'She shares the facilities,' Howard explained, meaning the bathroom. 'The trouble with houses in England, there are so few facilities,' he said. But this sharing meant that our three rooms were extraordinarily cheap; we had a sitting-room, a bedroom and a kitchen. There would be the extra strain of travelling for William but none for me. I thought this fair enough, starting, as I did, worse than I meant to go on. William didn't seem to mind this attitude. It actually made him happy.

We went out to dinner with Howard and Fred to seal the bargain. The Boys were enchanted to hear that William was almost a doctor, and lost no time in consulting him over dinner about their various ailments. William lost no time in switching the subject to music, referring to the musical articles he had read in the first two numbers of the *Highgate Review*.

Milly knew why I was leaving South Kensington. But she pretended not to know. She was happy with my promise to come and see her every Sunday. She said, 'It'll be better for your health, Nancy. All that travelling on the underground. And if William's with you, so much the better. It's awful the way that Isobel comes here to consult him, about to be a mother, and sitting up there in his room keeping him back from his studies.'

Isobel's new flat was off the Cromwell Road. In the past two weeks I would often find her when I got home in the evening sitting on William's bed, talking. I knew that he usually threw her out, for he was studying hard for his finals. But I was furious because she didn't for a moment think I could be the part of his life that I now was, and if she had realized it, she wouldn't have cared. She continued to think, speak and act as if I was motherly, and she was wrong as far as she was concerned. To be motherly, I felt, was her role.

One of the perquisites of the job which made life good for William and me were the occasional tickets we got for musical events that spring of 1955. William wrote a few short pieces for the *Highgate Review*, using his hours on the underground to do them. I begged Fred Tucher, who was in charge of this section, not to accept these pieces merely because William was my boyfriend, but he assured me William was both lucid and expert. Fred said many other good things about William, for Fred talked like the sea, in ebbs and flows each ending in a big wave which washed up the main idea. So that you didn't have to listen much at all, but just wait for the big splash. And so, from his long rippling eulogy I was able to report to William that his musical criticism was lucid and expert.

'Glad the Jessies approve,' William said. Jessies was his name for the Boys.

If in the early spring of 1955 you went to concerts at the Wigmore Hall, the Festival Hall, the Albert Hall and the smaller recital rooms of London, and Sadler's Wells and the Royal Opera House you must have seen the steamy and scruffy young couples and groups of eager young, sometimes on a cold night wearing woollen gloves and wrapped in scarves, waiting in queues for the cheap seats or hanging round the foyer. William and I were among them. When we didn't get tickets from the *Highgate Review* we bought them. *Don Giovanni* at Sadler's Wells; the Philharmonic Orchestra conducted by Otto Klemperer playing Mozart and Bruckner; at Conway Hall, Red Lion Square, an unknown string quartet gave us Tippett, Dvořák and Beethoven; *Daphnis and Chloë* at Sadler's Wells; at the Wigmore, Britten's *Three Canticles*; and I remember a charming piano and song recital at the Arts Council, though not the performers; *La Traviata* at Sadler's Wells.

'Do you have any religion, William?'

'No, I don't believe a damn thing.'

'I can't disbelieve,' I said.

'Well, you can go on believing for two, as the pregnant women eat.'

I was in no doubt that William was the love of my life. For his part he behaved as if our future together wasn't even in question. Looking back, it was good even then to have this area of certainty which in fact has never been shaken.

Our love affair in the basement at Highgate was strangely enhanced by the sterile affair going on upstairs between the kindly, well-informed and urbane Boys. Sometimes they came down and had a drink or supper with us, always anxious to consult William on medical matters. 'Of course I'm not qualified,' William said. 'I've never practised fully.'

William had been a poor boy. His origins were not merely of the working class with their pride and clean-scrubbed habits, their church-going. William came from the sub-poor. He was now the product of scholarships and bursaries, with a brain so exceptional that he had emerged from an infancy of dire want and wretched slum poverty without effort or much explanation. It was natural that good grammar schools and colleges of those days should take him up and want him as a pupil, that he should later travel to foreign universities on grants and scholarships, and enter the profession of his choice. He was now twenty-eight, already a cultivated man of easy humour. What moved and astonished me most was that he knew no nursery rhymes and fairy stories. He had read Dostoevsky, Proust, he read Aristotle and Sophocles in Greek. He had read Chaucer and Spenser. He was musical. He could analyse Shostakovich and Bartok. He quoted Schopenhauer. But he didn't know Humpty Dumpty, Little Miss Muffet, the Three Bears, Red Riding-Hood. He knew the story of Cinderella only through Rossini's opera. And all that sweet lyricism of our Anglo-Saxon childhood, a whole culture with rings on its fingers and bells on its toes, had been lost to him in that infancy of slums and smelly drains, rats and pawnshops, street prostitutes, curses, rags and hacking coughs, freezing bare feet and no Prince Charmings, which had still been the lot of the really poor in the years between the first and second world wars. I had never before realized how the very poor people of the cities had inevitably been deprived of their own simple folk-lore of childhood. At night, I used to sing nursery rhymes to William. I told him fairy stories. Occasionally one of them would vaguely recall to his mind something he had heard before, somewhere along the line. But most of them were quite new to him. They were part of our love affair.

I felt that any day Hector Bartlett would show up at the office in Highgate, if you could call such a cloudy decor of shell-pink and floral arrangements an office. Out of the way though we were, the magazine was now of sufficient importance and the personality of its editors magnetic enough to attract visitors who came without appointment, usually with manuscripts of essays or poems to offer. If neither Howard nor Fred was available, Abigail and I would give these visitors a cup of coffee and listen to them for half-an-hour. Sometimes people I had met in my previous jobs would turn up, which forced me to put aside the work mounting on my desk while we chatted about the same things as before. I would promise to bring their work to the attention of the editors while Abigail rattled busily at her mound of correspondence. Sometimes we were positively entertained. An interesting girl used to put in an appearance almost every week, dressed in different costumes; one week she was a milk-maid, another week a sort of cavalry officer. But she talked the same sense, evenly, all the time. Although she didn't manage to get her poems into the *Highgate Review*, I wasn't surprised when, many years later, she wrote a successful play.

Others came to discuss religion and to talk of their Anglo-Catholic retreats, and discuss the Thirty-nine Articles. The Anglo-Catholic movement at that time was in ferment over one particular subject: should they or shouldn't they 'go over to Rome'. Myself, I frequented both churches according as it suited me. When I revealed this fact to the religious intellectuals of the Highgate set, it never failed to lead to lengthy and fascinating discussions with no bearing whatsoever on the Christian faith.

So the spring passed. The manuscripts piled up on my desk and the letters on Abigail's, far more than she could manage. I helped her to open the mail in the mornings. Those letters which didn't appear to be urgent or personal for Howard Send or Fred Tucher bothered Abigail, not because she couldn't find anything to say to the writers but because there were so many. Fred had told her it would be 'nice' to reply to everyone, however hopeless or silly. So I told Abigail to work through them in such a way that they would be answered within quarterly intervals. And it is my advice to everyone with too much casual correspondence, to treat it in the same way that some companies pay their dividends. The mail that comes in before Christmas should be answered by Lady Day, the next pile by Midsummer Day, that accumulation by the Michaelmas term, and the last quarter by Christmas. It is the only proper system.

One morning the post held a manuscript with a covering letter from Hector Bartlett, enclosing a letter of recommendation from Emma Loy. 'It's from the pisser of prose,' said Abigail.

'I'll look at it later,' I said. Abigail went to put the large opened envelope containing the typescript and Emma Loy's letter on the pile of manuscripts on my desk. But, as if it were contagious, I took it out of Abigail's hand and put it down on the desk in a place by itself. I detested Hector Bartlett beyond all reasoning, but reasoning alone now began to justify my feelings.

Emma Loy's covering letter came from New York, thanking Fred Tucher for a copy of the *Highgate Review* which he had evidently sent her in the hope of persuading her to write something for it. 'I find it extremely interesting, especially as it is not available in this country,' wrote Emma. 'Be assured that if I have anything suitable to offer for publication I will send it to you.'

Now, I cannot remember word for word the text of this letter, written so long ago. But Emma went on something like this:

> I take this opportunity of recommending to you an article by the essayist Hector Bartlett which will accompany this letter. It describes an authentic experiment in the field of ESP and esoteric practises of that nature, under the specific heading of radionics. While I am not myself an adherent of the cult of radionics, Mr Bartlett, a convinced follower and student of radionic activities, describes an authentic experiment, the results of which cannot be ignored.
>
> In many ways Hector Bartlett may be described as 'the poor man's Kierkegaard'.
>
> The essay itself might need some editorial attention but the substance is, I think, worthy of your interest.
>
> Yours sincerely,
>> Emma Loy.

My feelings about Emma Loy at that moment, so far away in 1955, have been overlaid by later considerations, and my knowledge of how throughout her years of fame she was to be harassed and bothered continually by Hector Bartlett's writings about her, by his accounts of Emma Loy when he knew her, the falsities and the vaunted sensational revelations and the pathetic inventions. For when she finally cut him clean out of her life he was furious. As it happened nobody took much notice of what Hector Bartlett said. Emma was right not to sue and suppress, and waste her time with lawyers. 'I believe that's what he would like,' said Emma. 'It would draw attention to him.' But it annoyed her to see Hector Bartlett quoted by innocent students as one of the authorities on Emma Loy. And I think she knew she had only herself to blame through her persistence in those earlier years of trying to promote and appease him. Already, she was doing this with the idea of getting rid of him easier by making him out to be some sort of equal. It was perverse. More plainly than ever, she knew very well he was nothing more than the *pisseur de copie* that I called him.

So, at the time, I was enraged against Emma for her letter of recommendation. But the frightful essay of ten pages, unprintable though it was on literary grounds, and of insignificant interest from the general point of a good magazine, fascinated and chilled me so much that I wasn't able to think of anything else all day. Abigail, too, was astonished.

It was entitled *Radionics A Power Against Evil*. It gave a short explanation and history of the workings of the Box and its curative effects. Then came the case history which was the purpose of the essay. Hector Bartlett's claim was that the effectiveness of the Box depended on the sensitivity and psychic skill of the operator. These operators were at their best when directed by Organisers (his spelling). He went on to describe how an Organiser, knowing of an evil woman, had induced a naturally skilled operator to curse the evil one through the means of radionics. Since the victim of the curse was evil it was a benevolent accomplishment for the Organiser to induce the operator, a devout Catholic 'with all the psychic energy of her faith' to effect this curse. Within a few months of treatment, the evil victim, an extraordinarily obese woman, began to waste away and was unable to hold down a job.

Throughout the experiment, the essay explained, the Organiser had to work in very close and intimate cooperation with the operator which involved 'what might be termed a sexual-psychic relationship'. But the experiment was a success. In this case, the operator, apparently weakened in her powers by terror of the priesthood and her reputation amongst Catholics, had to be dropped from the programme and, incidentally, eventually went mad and committed suicide. But that in no way detracted from the obvious success of the experiment during the months that the operator came gradually under the full control of the Organiser. For future experiments it would probably be advisable to choose operators free from the oppressive influence of the mass-religions.

'He must mean Wanda Podolak,' said Abigail. 'Who is the poor fat woman?'

'Me,' I said.

'I don't remember you were so very fat.'

'I was when I first went to Mackintosh & Tooley. I started losing weight some time afterwards.'

'Yes, now I remember,' Abigail said. 'I didn't know you so well, then.'

She knew I always ate small portions but hadn't connected this with my now normal shape.

'If it's you, why does he think you're evil?'

'Because I met him in the park one morning last year when he was bothering me to do something about his career, and I called him to his face *pisseur de copie*.'

'He's bonkers,' said Abigail.

'I know, but Wanda's dead,' I said.

That night I took the letter of Emma Loy's and the article down to our basement flat to show William.

William had always been reserved about my hatred of Hector Bartlett. He felt, I think, that it was too personal. It is possible that William wanted all my strong feelings, of whatever sort, for himself. Not long before, I had told him patiently about the connection I felt sure existed between Hector and Wanda's death, the logical sequence. 'He came to the house always when I was at work. I suppose he slept with her. He taught her to work the Box under his influence, and induced her to work it against me,' I said.

'Oh, God,' said William. 'Even if it's all true you still can't say the man drove her to suicide. It takes two to make that sort of relationship. It's a pact between the oppressor and the oppressed. Whatever she did she must have wanted to.'

But I had pressed on. Wanda was under his influence and when she wanted to stop he showed her the fake press-cuttings and some no doubt obscene faked-up photographs. And it was just too much. She gave her long desperate scream and jumped into the canal.

'Wouldn't stand up in a court of law,' said William. He was tough; but he was also tough on himself.

Now I took Hector's essay to show him. 'It's all there,' I said.

First he read Emma's letter. '. . . poor man's Kierkegaard . . .' was his comment. 'The poor man doesn't need a Kierkegaard, he needs a job.'

'Read that essay,' I ordered. – 'Essay so-called.'

He put it aside. 'Later on,' he said. 'Come on, Mrs Hawkins, I'll take you out to supper.' (William still gives me the 'Mrs Hawkins' from time to time, as when he says, 'I'll have a bit less of your advice, Mrs Hawkins.')

There was a great row going on upstairs when we got back. It wasn't the first time since we had come to live in the basement that our nights had been disturbed by the raised voices of Howard and Fred, in the daytime so mild and sweet to each other and everybody. Mrs Thomas, the cleaning lady, came out of her room. 'The Boys are at it again,' she said. 'This time it sounds bad. Should we go up?'

'No, don't interfere,' said William.

'Doesn't it disturb your studies?' said Mrs Thomas, who was really looking for company in the crisis, much as people had gathered together during the war, under the bombs.

'I've studied through worse rackets,' said William, firmly shutting our door behind us.

Perhaps it was the fact that homosexual practices were still against the law that made homosexuals in those days much more hysterical than they are now. The screaming emotions from upstairs were far worse than usual tonight, and it was clear that objects were being thrown about both in the sitting-room and in the office above our heads. They were now having a real fight, with thuds and shouts and the crash of glass.

'Shouldn't we try to stop them?' I said.

'It's no good at the moment,' said William with his street-savvy. 'You have to wait for a lull. You then go in and start shouting yourself.'

'Call the police?'

'The police will come anyway if they go on like this.'

Someone bounded down the basement steps and banged at our door. It was Fred, the younger partner, his handsome brown face smeared with blood. 'We need a doctor,' he said. 'Howard has collapsed. He hurt his leg.'

We went up, with Mrs Thomas in the wake. Howard had not hurt his leg, he had some broken ribs. He lay on the carpeted floor of the office, moaning. 'Don't worry,' Fred told him. 'We have a doctor in the house.'

'Who's going to clean all this up?' said Mrs Thomas.

We got Howard into hospital in an ambulance and put plasters on Fred's face. The office was completely wrecked, with manuscripts torn and watery from overturned flower-vases. The typewriters were somewhere in the street having been heaved through the window. Nobody asked for or gave a single explanation.

It was a week before we could set up the office again. The *Highgate Review* was held up for two months. Abigail and I pieced together some of the typescripts and proofs and wrote apologies to the authors we could trace, explaining there had been an accident, begging them to re-submit their work.

But most of the papers were irretrievable, soaked, and

trampled to shreds. We swept up the sodden mess over the weekend and threw it all out. William gave us a hand .

'The thing about the Boys,' I remember Abigail saying, 'they're basically charming. When homosexuals are charming it sugars the pill.'

Howard, home from hospital, was in bed in his room above the office, and Fred was mildly carrying on with his work, his affable meetings and his flower arrangements. William and I stayed on in the basement till just before Christmas when we were married, and there were no more disturbances. 'The fight to end fights,' said William.

But in that first week when Abigail and I, with the help of Mrs Thomas, the carpenters and glaziers, were putting things straight and searching for lost letters and manuscripts, it was in our own flat that I searched the most. The article by Hector Bartlett and Emma Loy's letter had completely disappeared.

'I brought them down here, what did you do with them, William?' I finally said, for I knew he must have put them somewhere.

'I took them back up to the office the morning after the fight, and dumped them among the wreckage,' William said. 'That's where they belonged.'

'Why did you do that?'

'We don't have room for rubbish like that down here.'

I went to console Howard in his bed of pain among his flowers. 'It's all straight down there, now,' I said. 'Only we've lost nearly all the letters and manuscripts.'

'We'll get more, I guess,' said Howard.

'Look,' I said, 'there was a letter from Emma Loy. She hadn't anything to offer herself, but she sent an essay on radionics by an author called Hector Bartlett. It's lost, and so is the letter.'

'What's radionics?'

'A sort of witchcraft,' I said. 'The essay was no good. Have you heard of Hector Bartlett?'

'No,' he said.

'He's a *pisseur de copie*,' I said.

'Jesus, please don't make me laugh,' said dear Howard, holding his poor ribs.

14

Later that year, when we were planning the wedding, I lay awake for a while, then drowsily falling asleep I thought how Wanda could make my dress, until I remembered she was dead.

More than thirty years later, I saw Hector Bartlett again. It was in Tuscany in a restaurant that had been constructed within a restored medieval castle famous for Dante's having once slept there. It was about three in the afternoon. We had finished our lunch. William had to go and make a promised phone call to England, where the time was then two o'clock. We often go to Italy. That afternoon, the Italian voices lilted the doings of the day. The sun blazed outside, Apollo as he is, on the wine- and oil-soaked skins of our friends and fellows who set off with great cheer in their Alfas, their Fiats and their Lancias. William said, 'You pay the bill. I'll make that call.'

I paid the bill, waited for the change, and set off towards the door. The serving counter was surrounded by people, mostly visiting English. A voice said something about its being a lovely place. Another voice replied, 'Yes, there's a wealth of wild flowers and butterflies.' Something about the tourist-brochure quality of the phrase made me look at the speaker. Thin, with a grey face and white wispy hair, it was, after all these years, Hector Bartlett. He noticed my searching look, and staring back, recognized me. I believe some of the people around him were friends or travelling acquaintances in his group. He looked at them then back at me, and started to laugh nervously.

'*Pisseur de copie*,' I hissed.

He walked backwards so that the people behind him had to make way for him, still with his short staccato laugh like a typewriter.

William was waiting for me at the car.

'Did you settle the bill?' he said.

I said, 'Yes.'

It was a far cry from Kensington, a far cry.